# FLOAT

# FLOAT

## an Anthology of New Writings
## 2024

*"She waited for the train to pass. Then she said,
'I sometimes think that people's hearts are like
deep wells. Nobody knows what's at the bottom.
All you can do is imagine by what comes
floating to the surface every once in a while.'"*
~ Haruki Murakami

# Contents

## Amy Han
### Founder, Words of a Feather

Somewhere in the midst of 2023, I took a long break. It had been over a decade since I'd quit a full-time job to pursue my dream of not only writing, but sharing my love of writing by leading workshops for young people. Within this time, my personal life had shifted many times over. The business grew, in more wonderful and exciting ways than I could have imagined. Like a child, it became its own entity, evolving to have an identity of its own. There was one studio, then two, then Covid came along, and none. We were online only, then trying to be what we were in a world that was not as it was. I was not who I was (or perhaps I was finally becoming who I had always been). I knew something had to change. I had opened this studio - originally named Creative Write-it - for the kid-version of me who would have loved to have been part of it. I still loved (love!) working with kids, but I missed attending workshops and events for adult me.

Hence, the long break. I've been lucky enough to have spent many months over the last few years in Paris, a literary arts hub if there ever was one. Every night, it seems there are workshops, gatherings, or spoken word nights; there are bookshops, libraries, and cafés that invite long stretches of writing and people-watching on every corner. The Parisian-style apartment buildings, gothic and medieval monuments, and cobblestone laneways are heavy with *histoires*. The City of Lights is just as accurately a City of Rats, and even this lends itself to a writer's brain. Here, I remembered what it was to *be a writer* (not only a business owner who writes and teaches writing) - wandering, wondering, paying attention, inspired. During my long break, Creative Write-it was reborn as Words of a Feather (WOAF).

There were so many new ideas that I wanted to offer, inspired by my time in Paris as well as what I craved to attend as a creative myself. I dreamed up a "Creativity Picnic" - a gathering in which people could meet in a park and *create*, in any way, quietly, for a solid amount of time before sharing a pot-luck lunch. I wanted to offer an open mic event ("Story Soirées") where readings and performances were invited by anyone who felt brave enough to share - polished and unpolished work welcome. There was an idea for a monthly Flash Fiction competition, weekly gatherings to encourage a regular practice, and more.

In late 2023, the magic of the Instagram algorithm introduced me to The Provocative Inklings (PI). From their page, I gathered that they were a passionate group of arts students and emerging writers who wanted to *do things* in the Melbourne literary scene. As a UniMelb graduate from many moons ago, it felt serendipitous to be connected back to this place that I had come from. We messaged, and met, and wrote together. I had all of these ideas, and so many years of experience, but knew I couldn't bring WOAF to life as I was dreaming of it without others who were fuelled by a similar dream. The Inklings were looking for mentorship and a framework to gain momentum as a literary collective. I think both WOAF and PI would have grown even if we hadn't met - Angus and Kartiya of the Inklings certainly never needed me to make many of the leaps and bounds that they have made, as PI and as individual writers, since we met. But I'm sure those ideas of mine wouldn't have taken off the way they have over the last year without them. I am so grateful for the crossing of our paths, for the community we have gathered and continue to build together. I'm so grateful for you, dear readers, contributors, artists, and supporters of the written and spoken word, who have in some way or another, found us.

This anthology, *FLOAT*, was an idea I spoke to Angus about one evening in July. By midnight, we had our theme. By the end of the week, we announced that we would be publishing a book and opened submissions.

I can't tell you how moved I have been to read each of the contributions to this book. Each of these authors have participated in a WOAF and/or PI workshop, competition, or event; many have participated in multiple ways over this first year of ours as WOAF, and as collaborators with PI. We are so excited to celebrate this year with the most timeless and tangible of ways of honouring writing: a 'real', published book.

Within these pages, you'll find poetry, short stories, flash fiction, and creative non-fiction/memoir. From a hot-air balloon in the sky to the floating skin of a lake, each of these writings are transportive, immersive, dreamy, and deeply moving, in their own ways.

Writers, thank you so much for entrusting us with your work.

I'm so glad you found us, and that you are holding this book in your hands. From a writer with big dreams, as I believe we all are, this means the world.

It is truly a dream and an honour to have edited and put this anthology together; to have been carried along these streams of words like driftwood; and to be able to share these writings with you.

Who knows where the winds will take us next. The journey is as exciting as any result.

Best wishes,
Amy

# *Angus Clark*
## *Co-founder, The Provocative Inklings*

I slaved away at university doing a BA with a creative writing major. I was always asked that condescending, sometimes genuinely curious question, "and where will that take you in life?"

This answer changed to fit the scene, and I have a rather long list of template answers for you. But sitting at uni during Covid, during sort-of-Covid and then 'post'-Covid, I saw the gaping holes in the creative community for writers. I saw that many people did not think they were a writer. I saw many people resigning to write merely as a hobby. I mean no disrespect to the joys of hobby, but I observed people who wanted it to be more than a hobby. As I went along in my degree I became increasingly *laissez-faire* towards it, especially as my eyes, mind and heart turned to the case of creativity. I couldn't wait to get out. In my excellent time in Melbourne, this literary city, this city of festivals, I have talked to baristas, uni students, passersby, old people, young people and more who yearn to write more. It really was a no-brainer when Kartiya and I decided to co-found The Provocative Inklings - with the rigorous support of our friends Lachlan and Amy - and contribute directly to the solution we had in mind. This was, as it turns out, creating space through events for creative writers and artists to mingle, to showcase and to be inspired by each other and their work.

Little did I know this would ignite a passion for being the events man in my diverse projects. Even in my paid work now, interning with an excellent group called Solution Entertainment. Creativity is beautiful in every form, but the priority of it when money is drying up shrinks and shrinks. But the cry for it rises higher and higher. Through The Provocative Inklings, I am so proud and grateful to be helping us all to keep those creative events alive. So much of what we have done has also been in the spirit of collaboration. Amy - Words of a Feather - has been our dear friend, mentor and close collaborator for so much of the journey, and we hope this remains into the future. This was never going to be a singular journey, but I am grateful that the people I am taking it with are the likes of Amy and Kartiya, whose passion and ideas for the writing arts takes us to new places. I am grateful for the contributors to this very fine anthology, and the people who fill our events. We are all writers and artists, and we will thrive together.

What is the next door hiding for us? I couldn't say. But gosh I'm excited to open it. The next step. The next idea. The next event. Melbourne is our playground, my friends. A storied page to write on. A busy wall to throw a tag onto. A giant cafe to drink its coffee in. Write it all down.

Stay Provocative,
Angus Clark, an Inkling

# *Kartiya Ilardo*
# *Co-founder, The Provocative Inklings*

My creative journey has been more of a life-changing, identity-shaping one.

I was just starting my Masters in Teaching at the University of Melbourne. However, I always wanted to be a writer ... an artist. I let that fall to the wayside because I believed it would be a hard industry to break into, and who would want to read what I had to say? Who was I to take up space? But writing always seemed to find a way to creep back into my life. I did my undergraduate degree at the University of Melbourne planning to originally major in Psychology, but after my first year, I heard the calling of writing... creative writing. In my first creative writing class, I met Angus. For the next few classes, over the three year degree, I kept on fatefully bumping into Angus. I finished with my degree, majoring in both Psychology and Creative Writing, and went straight on to my Masters. But I still felt inadequate. Again, who am I to take up space?

First semester into my degree, I was sitting in on a lecture and I get a notification. Angus. We hadn't talked for a while. He invited me and a few more of his writing friends to have a writer catch-up; nothing serious, just lighthearted writing. This reignited me. I would wake up at 5:00 am and catch the earliest train just to meet them in the mornings at Brunetti before my classes and talk about writing. They were the highlights of my week, and I never could have dreamed what it has become and what it is becoming.

Fast forward a few months and we've created a thriving community, with the help of so many other creatives like the wonderful Amy Han of Words of a Feather. Many of you are in this book or reading it or both — hello!

Creating with Angus and Amy has helped me blossom into the person I am today. It has reignited the creative spirit within me. Alongside sparking my inner writer and film-maker, I've come to appreciate the beauty of dance, something which came into my life by surprise and swept me off my feet. Whatever your creative style is, with what we are doing, we are capturing moments; creating tapestries of moments in time. My piece, which you'll read in this book, captures a very special moment for me. With poetry, its life its vibrancy is forever alive. As artists, we observe the atmosphere, the people, the environment, the reactions, and feelings. For me, creating makes you appreciate the life you've been given.

The bittersweet reality is that every moment is fleeting, forever slipping through our hands like sand. But through writing, we are allowed to hold on longer, even if it's just for a little bit.

— Kartiya

# 1

## *Callum Mintzis*

## HERE, THERE IS NO TIME

A crop of wheat lies naked to the sun, her gentle eyes conversing with the hills and the birds. Children ride bicycles, as bells ring for the cattle calling home. Laughter sings to the rivers, and the sweet breeze replies. The cobbles lay in rows, holding up the carts and animals, peoples and their pride. There, a sparrow walks and sees that here, there is no time.

Two birds play as lovers to the paddocks, their eyes met by the same green in which they fall, dancing to the dreaming of the winds. Clouds elope with the seasons. They travel together, pouring themselves for the birth of trees, birds, and rivers. Bowing humbly in apology, the clouds move on. A court of foxes wade through thickets of long, green grass, with their heads soaring higher than the grass itself. Here, there is no time.


***Callum Mintzis*** *is a composer, performer, writer and psychotherapist based in Melbourne, Australia. His work is informed by a deep passion for the nature of life itself, and the integral value of each human being's individual experience.*

# 2

# *A.C. Perri*

## REMNANTS OF US – PART I

Further out, outside that which is consciously known, yet, not logically founded—

the other side from where we all gathered, once, shall I be again known to you.

There comes a time, an hour, a second, in which your pain and joys shall haphazardly be packaged into one great painful bundle for you to unfurl. Though a mind escapes you, the vile thoughts not your own, if for only a minute, the damage is done, fulfilled in the prophecy of self until the overflow of sadness takes hold of your mind. Did you think once, you are the imposter hosting an original to claim along your way out? Have you caught yourself seeking the freedoms of childhood, filled with the visions that explored dark secrets? The best version of you kidnapped by strangers visiting your own mind.

Are you aware we are all kept anchored to this world by a silver chord while the physical vessel slumbers?

Prey we have all become, surviving in a mattered version of ourselves, constantly treading the waters of turmoil, resisting their advances put before you. Your life's journey, Titanic proportions heading straight for the iceberg, the compass forever stuck on disaster. From shadowy enigmas visiting you while dreaming, day-drifting from dimensions to realms crossing dilapidated bridges to other worlds, did you know you are being hunted?

# REMNANTS OF US – PART II

Do not show them your intentions when you go observing those parts of the universe deemed dark matter, don't seek their assistance, nor obey their false instructions for there are no directions nor global positioning systems to these destinations only the desire to be freed from the ethos of matter, the traditions and customs of being born into flesh suit. You have free will to choose, a spirit so great that they must restrain you with fear and hate. Know your own strength, rise to their challenge, there is not one person living or breathing that needs them.

Abandon the falsehoods they force unto you, know you are stronger, so much more powerful than all the screens that make up the entire modern world you currently live in. Your shoes though worn, do not need mending, the soles can carry you a lot further by will only. Forget the snowstorms and hail which come at you, do not stop because of the rain, merely individual droplets gathered together to cause havoc. Be certain to know that your true compass is deep in your heart of hearts; when you leave this place of mayhem and doom, look down as you float upwards at the turmoil beneath you, know that you are on the right path, back on your journey, the one you started long ago, but were interrupted with the noise of humanity, known you are being guided back to your true home.

## OF IMAGINED BEINGS

The night you came to be me, like dust on a whisper, you floated in on a breeze, gathered and swirled until the form came about. You imagined so strong your desire as pure as the thought in a newborn's mind, finally settled where I had once called my place. Histories and tragedies, pile high to the heavens, then gone in a blink, the eye of the beholder the only true witness. Your essence blown into corners without escape ladders, you gather the ashes spread out to the masses, your presence that of sandstorms eroding the desert goes forth. Barren all has become, for time is the master, the imposter of time-keeping floating on a whim of other's desires, imaginations running wild, havoc is their creations born out of desperation.

The old world is erased through a flood of some sort, too great the shock, we can only remember now again; *Déjà vu* the hint, comes visiting while we think of familiar scents, nostalgia grounded into our bones, the fine powder found in our long-forgotten memory cells. Placed under deep slumber, embraced in protection from the celestial mother, her dear children, lost, taken by the trickster now in command. Know you are watched as the seconds on a clock, for you are the cup half filled with calm liquid, the spark which starts off lightning, the sound of loud thunder on a cloud-free day; the hum of the bees keeping them afloat, the sweet elixir of life landing on one's tongue... the freedom of taste floating into mouths hungry for love.


*A.C. Perri has been writing free-style poetry and pieces of fiction described as 'delightfully unconventional' and 'over-the-top' creative works for many years. She has won awards for her work having had a few published in Indie magazines.*

# 3

# *Jason Schembri*

## LAKESKIN

This was no ordinary lake—the stories had that much right. A thin layer of skin stretched over the surface of the water, delicate film streaked in angry veins like the wings of a dragonfly. Reeds swayed lakeside, and it was impossible to tell if they were beckoning me closer or warning me away.

Memories, keen and biting, lanced the membrane of my mind. I waded through them all, trying not to look too hard, trying not to remember anything in particular: not the baritone croon of her voice, nor the way her skin felt on mine, silk against silk, slipping and falling and sinking, nor the taste—

A damselfly caught my attention, dancing just above the lake's surface with a deliberate grace. For a moment it seemed to hesitate, as if suddenly aware of its own reflection in the dark water below. Then, without warning it dropped head-first, plunging itself to its own demise. The surface rippled momentarily, then stilled.

Dusk fell at once, dropping fractured light across the gossamer lake, and I lowered my gaze to my own rippled reflection. Had I always been so damned pale? Ringlets knotted and torn, sickly bones threatening to penetrate my skin. I looked more corpse than person. How could she have ever loved me?

I dropped onto the bank and pushed my knees into the soft earth, staining the hem of my dress. The crude scent of soil rose up to meet me. A memory pushed to the surface and I heard myself whimper. I placed my hand in the lake, tearing the film and dipping my fingers in the frigid water: a welcome pain. Images flooded my mind in stark torrents as I let go, more memories surrendered to the lake. I relished the space they left behind, a numb bliss at the base of my skull.

The water embraced me as I stepped in. Nearby, the reeds trembled against one another in applause, their spindly forms sinister in the fading light. I lay on my back in the shallow water and pushed off the bank with my bare feet. The lake's skin gave way as I glided through the murk, staring up at the darkening sky. I stopped in the heart of the lake, my hair drifting around me like a dark halo. I imagined I looked like a pale saint, shivering through a baptism of ice.

I could already feel the lake's mysteries at work. My mind was clearing; memories of *her* carried away with the white mist I exhaled in quick shivers. I closed my eyes. A swathe of lakeskin brushed against my leg and I kicked it away. The faint buzz of an insect cut through the silence overhead.

As the memories of her passed through me they grazed my consciousness, coming back to me in echoes. Out of nowhere and without warning, I felt her lips on mine, but when I opened my eyes I saw nothing but the mist. Then the memory turned to smoke, a thin wisp escaping my throat and out into the ether. My lips, another barren space where passion once lay.

*What was her name?* The thought came to me in a panic, and I had to remind myself where I was, what I was doing.

The buzzing grew louder and its source blew into my vision. A small dragonfly, blood-red and bloated. It moved in wild skitters then paused in the air as if held there, observing me. I must have seemed a queer anomaly, an unnatural trespasser floating in its home. Without a second thought it left me, skimming the surface of the lake as it went, not looking back as it disappeared through the mist.

Another memory weeded out and uprooted: her eyes, cold and unforgiving, frozen in time and watching me with curiosity. But how those eyes came alive at night, burned bright when I told her my darkest secrets! They searched me over, as if I held the answers to all her questions. They drank me in, as if I were her sustenance. *Were they blue, or were they grey?*

A cry escaped my frozen lips. She was almost gone from me entirely.

I lifted my head. The lake around me shimmered now, drenched in a sheet of silver moonlight. Only one memory left, a vision of skin and fabric. I tried to beg, to scream, *just this one, please, just leave me this and take the rest,* but all I managed was a sick gurgle of bile.

The lakeskin tore as I kicked and reached out for the bank, which was somewhere beyond the mist. My hands seized as I cut through the surface, and it was near impossible to focus on the reeds beyond the slick water. I was too far from shore—the memory had already begun to fade.

I looked down into the murk below and plunged, spiralling down into the abyss. Thunder rushed my ears as I scrabbled over dark shapes amongst the sediment at the bottom of the lake. My feet found purchase beneath a curved piece of hardwood. I ran my hands over the silt, my fingers finding smooth stones of odd shapes and sizes. I filled the pockets of my dress.

The memory was still there, a fragment of a fragment—it was safe with me down here. My dress sagged in the current, coaxing me down. My fingers were still in my pockets, and I realised that some of the stones weren't stones at all. Small, fractured bones, different shapes and sizes.

Then came the burning. It tore through my chest, heaving convulsions wrenching my body. My lungs thrashed within, yet I braced myself against the need. My arms reached up in a brief remnant of primal instinct and I urged them back. They drifted down like fallen debris, dropping to my sides.

I searched for the last memory and held it close. I could see it now. She lay on the bed, her body draped in a pool of silk sheets, skin painted blue in the soft midnight glow. It was just an image, but it would have to be enough.

My skin tingled, a pleasant kind of numbness, though my lungs still seized with fury. I peered through the murky water at the vague figures around me, shapes revealing themselves with sickening clarity. Bodies, dozens of them, all frozen in icy decay, heads tilted up to the surface.

*What's wrong?* she had asked me, her lips pressing a firm line in the darkness. Her hands had found mine, pulling me close.

*Bad dream.* I had said. I could smell her still, the scent of home. *I was dying, I couldn't breathe. And you weren't there.*

She'd held me close to her chest then. I'd never known warmth like that, before or since.

The fire left my lungs, extinguished by mouthfuls of viscous water. My body ceased its struggle and I stared up at the still surface. A tear in the skin above offered a brief glimpse of sky: indifferent clouds floating by a lonely moon.

*I'll always be here, my love.* Her lips had brushed against my neck, and in response I shivered at the bottom of the lake. Her embrace had been so tight, so sure, that in that moment, I had truly believed her. *You'll never be alone.* I closed my eyes and came to rest amongst the corpses and sediment, and for that moment, everything was perfect.


**Jason Schembri** *is a queer Melbourne-based writer with a hunger for exploring identity, history, and the darker side of humankind. His writing often straddles the nebulous line between literary and speculative fiction. His bio remains his most elusive piece to date.*

# 4

## *Ethan Upfold Wood*

## DINING TABLE VIGNETTE

Biting down on the encrusted mango, the mandibles smacked it to a pulp. Sugar licked off lips, he squinted at the speckled bananas bathed in the window's sunlight. Through the blur, a speckle whirred and became still, uneasily drifted, and again settled. An onion like a great brown French sun sat before the gaunt motions moving back and forth through the labile *mise-en-scène*. The slicked lips were once more sprinkled by the dried flesh fed through to the arcade's procession.

# YUTORI

White paper spilled my form
       mangled rings complete
arranged in space
with note and pen

nick sings a mustard seed
the cup is empty

pink paper held firm
its ordered intricacies
kept me awake

slung again
over the road between
unsettled at home

time by paged line
a sick week slug
above the street
falling down slowly
hoping to take flight

# REMEDIAL DANCE

H and in hand
        circling laughter in song
a playground or was it
tunnelled classroom, blurry warm
lined jackets on hooks
clothed pigeonholes

a door's sharp rap
insidious agents creep
stalk me              as I lay sleeping
mine own terrors

that black foot
crosses the landing        into the spell
take Nick Cave's hand
among accumulated pixels

spin with us
re-drum the door

we spin and circle      circle and spin
fading further adrift
our unbroken spell
Remedial Dance

**E.U. Wood** *is a student and writer hailing from West Melbourne. Among other topics, they enjoy observing the small details of ordinary life in writing.*

# 5

# *Sara Rose Oliver*

## MOONFLOWER

A young girl rises from the soil of a desolate planet. Iridescent moonflowers surround her body, each stem tucked into the world with buried secrets and forgotten promises. The flowers glimmer and pulse in the gentle winds, folding into the girl's long hair as she reaches her hand to the stars and notices their foreign shapes.

She cannot remember her name or which letters are supposed to curl and drag over a vacant page. She was told that a name is unneeded when there is no reason to be called for. Yet, she knows she is meant to be here.

The field stretches into a perpetual darkness overgrown with grass and moon vine. A light vanilla scent permeates the air, settling her rapid heart with a stroke of familiarity. She wears the same cotton ivory dress decorated in the memory of her first oil painting, the stains now fading into patterns too perfect to be born from misfortune.

The moonflowers swish in the quiet night, granting the young girl's oldest wish—solitude. She had often dreamed of pouring the ink of her youth into a small jar, but it had dried out by the time she finally found it again.

As she sifts through the flower field scratching her small limbs on each petal, a note flutters from her pocket. She reads the dainty handwriting, marked with smudged ink.

*Find the red flower and you will be free.*

For a moment, she is thankful to be gifted purpose in a world so empty. With purpose comes liberation, and yet also an undeniable sense of vulnerability. She does not want any stitches to be unravelled when there is nobody to blame for her undoing. Nobody but herself.

The girl stretches her gaze to each corner of the world with a sigh laced with defeat. A sea of moonflowers rolls in to the eternity before her. She does not remember the last time she felt sunrays against her pale skin; she only knows the deep companionship of a dark abyss. It may have been days now, or even decades. She soon learns that her body will not need sustenance of any kind, and that time moves differently in this world.

In an entire universe, the girl has been crafted only to belong here. Alone. Alone until she cannot remember what it means to have her frosty cheeks cupped in warm hands, or fingertips tracing her naked spine. Alone until she has forgotten the concept of familiarity. Alone until her heartbeat is only dependant on the number of stars in the sky or the patter of rain against her skin. Until she thinks she can see a trumpet-shaped flower burning like an ember in the dark. But it is not red she sees, only an old dream poking through the holes of her reality.

*Find the red flower and you will be free.*

The note has faded into few decipherable letters, but she has repeated the phrase so many times that it no longer matters. It has been tattooed across her soul. The girl has begun to wonder what freedom truly means but at least knows she has left something behind. She can feel it when she stares so long that the flowers wilt and cry for help. It's as if she never existed anywhere but here. She has left her name somewhere in the stars, somewhere she can no longer reach and with it, a woman who never gave the girl inside of her a chance to be set free.

The moonflowers pull the stars into the soil as they glow, incandescent bubbles against the night's vast shadows. Their petals float like atoms as she dances through this wonderous night with a newfound determination, but her choreographed steps soon turn to shuffles in the grass and for the first time, she wonders if it will ever truly end.

A transient figure floats before her. As she draws closer, the girl can slightly make out the features of a much older woman. Its wrinkles sag with the grief of lost time, its spine hunched over, weakened by gravity. The girl avoids looking at the shadow's eyes for too long as she feels it carving lessons in her unscathed heart. Yet, she is somehow relieved that she has not been alone all this time.

"Have you seen a red flower?" the young girl asks, but the shadow's face is covered in tears as she murmurs something to the wind.

The girl never saw the shadow again but searched for it every night, even between the flowerbeds and the constellations. She couldn't go on after seeing such pain from such a familiar face. As more time passes, the girl can feel her fingers shaking the longer she looks, her long hair fading into a stark white. She can feel herself shrinking into the earth until suddenly she becomes a part of the soil, and her body is cradled in a field of moonflowers.

"I'm sorry," she whispers to the wind, a final tear slipping from her cheek.

A red flower blossoms.

*Sara Rose Oliver (23) is an emerging writer from Melbourne, Australia who specialises in conceptualising abstract ideas through creative mediums such as music, writing and painting. She is currently studying Professional Writing and Editing at RMIT.*

# 6

# Joseph Langley

## WEIGHTLESS

*content warning: suicidality, depression*

Agirl sat on the sagging roof of a humble cabin and wished that she could see the stars. The woods were thick, and the canopy thicker; not a blotch of the sky shone through. She had never fallen in all the thousands of times she had sat there, and yet her mother thought she might every time. She also had never floated up above the trees, but her mother never worried about that.

The girl's only companion on that roof was an instrument, which she played without looking down from the canopy. She played without using her hands, either– and indeed she played without using any physical part of herself. The instrument had a wide array of strings, pulled taught along a graceful neck which arched above a basin of water. It was with her *mind* that the girl played those strings; she plucked individual droplets of water up from the basin, Connecting to them and making them float.

See, there was a reason that her mother might have worried that this girl would float away above the trees. Yet despite the girl's best efforts, she had never before managed to make *herself* float.

Footsteps, on the shingles behind her. She still didn't look down, but she did reach over and rest a hand on the instrument. The floating water slammed upward at greater a pace, blaring the melody louder.

"Selena," said a voice from behind her, in a tone that betrayed the great effort it took to remain steady. A hand rested on Selena's shoulder. "Come on. Don't you want dinner?"

Selena kept the music blaring.

"Selena, you *have* to be getting hungry. You've been up here for hours."

"What do you want, mamma?" She let all the water fall down into the basin, shrugging off her mum's hand. The canopy felt farther without music.

"I just want you to come inside," her mother grabbed the instrument, tried to pull it away. "Come on."

Selena wrenched back. "You just want to take dad away from me."

Her mother, who Selena could now see after being forced to face her from the struggle over the instrument, stiffened. Her face was lined beyond her years, and her entire demeanor sagged with a heaviness at odds with her frailty.

But frailty becomes jagged when rubbed against the wrong way. "I never said that," she whispered, yanking on the instrument harder. "Give it to me, you've lost it for the week."

Selena staggered, trying to hold on, leaning back to put all her weight into the pull–

She screamed as it slipped from her mother's grip and she fell towards the edge–

Her mother caught her arm, but the instrument's momentum carried it over. Selena threw out a hand, leaning over the abyss.

Far below, the ground swam in her vision. She Connected to the instrument even as it fell, and it stopped falling. It floated. Right up to her outstretched hand. Her mother yanked her back, gripping her arm tight.

"It's too easy for you to Connect with that thing," she whispered.

Selena shrugged off her mother's grip, but followed her to the side window and climbed back into her room behind her mother. "Is it so bad that I remember the good things about him too, mamma?"

Her mother closed her window with agonising movements, pulling the latch, and pressing down on all the corners of the jamb to make sure that not a crack remained open. Her veins stood out against her thin wrists. "Just keep the window shut for me okay?" She took the instrument from Selena's hands, who resisted for a short time, before the broken look in her mother's eyes weakened her fingers.

Selena folded her arms and sat on her bed, watching her mom leave. As soon as the door shut behind her, Selena huffed and Connected to the window. All it took was the slightest tug inside herself; she had touched the latch a thousand times with her hand, knew the smooth cold metal against her palm, knew the lingering smell it left on her fingers. The tip of the latch floated, pulling up to undo the lock. The window floated, cracking open, letting in a calming breeze.

She took a small and savage thrill of power from the success, and settled in to wait. No way would she go downstairs for food, it didn't matter how hungry she was. That would be admitting defeat.

She was in the midst of Connecting to her pillow, watching it float to the ceiling, and letting it fall back to bounce off her head, when her room grew darker. She turned to the window.

A dark and miasmic *something* crawled through the open crack. She screamed, leaping forward and slamming the window shut. It bisected the thing, sending half of it collapsing to her floor in a writhing heap. Water, she realised, though it moved like it was alive, forming pseudopods and feelers that snaked across the ground–

"MAMMA," she screamed, running out of her room and slamming the door shut. "MAMMA!" She ran down the rickety stairs.

The fire roared, heat suffusing the humble room that served as both their kitchen and their den. The trunk of their host tree grew through the floor in the far corner, holding the weight of their entire abode. Any cracks that would open into the outside world– around the base of the tree, in slats of wood– were stuffed with old linens. Her mother wept by the water tap that ran out from the tree trunk, trying to shove a dirty rag up to plug the hole–

"Selena t-the cloth won't, it won't stay–"

"I've got it mamma," she stumbled next to her mother, reaching out and feeling the dirty cloth between her fingers. Each grain of old dirt and snot, the slight sticky edges of it– her mother had used this as a handkerchief, clearly just making do with whatever she had–

In that realization, Selena Connected to it and made it float. It jammed up into the spigot, sealing it shut.

"Mamma, *what's happening–*" the house shook, every window blotted dark by streaks of water running *up* the outside walls. Her mother gathered her into her arms, squeezing her tight.

"It's okay Selena, it's okay, it'll all be okay–" but her words sounded like they were meant for herself, and not Selena. "It's okay... it's okay..."

Through slow and bated breaths, the house stopped shaking. The streaks of water outside stopped flowing.

"I think he's gone away now," she whispered. "I think he's gone away."

Selena stiffened, but her mother didn't seem to notice, rubbing Selena's back, whispering into her ear.

"He never showed you his Connection, you know– he told me he didn't want you to see him as inhuman, or strange, so he always stayed corporeal for you... but I know the real reason Selena, he didn't want you to know like I did how he could sneak into places and steal things, destroy things...

there's nothing better at seeping and destroying than water, it's almost impossible to keep it out..."

Selena shook in her mother's arms, staring over her shoulder, eyes distant.

"I know you still love him Selena," her mother whispered. "I know you do. It's so hard, because you know, a part of me does too... Sometimes I catch myself staring into my cups, staring at the water I'm about to drink, and thinking about his laugh... it always sounded so swirly and bubbly, like water... but then when I hear his laugh in my head, Selena I can't tell if it's the laugh he used to give while we lay on the roof together, staring at the canopy, or if it's the little chuckle he gave to try and lighten the blow when he told me he wasn't sure if he loved me anymore, a-and I don't know if all of this obsessive thinking of mine is love or resentment or whether the two are really any different–"

"Mamma–"

"Now he's just here for you," she whispered. "And I can't let him in because he's just here for you, the daughter he never got to see grow up because he sunk that ship a long time ago, but I don't think he cares Selena, I think he'll do anything–"

"Mamma what if he's not so bad?" Selena whispered. "I remember his laugh too, I miss his laugh Mamma..."

Something clunked on the stairs, but neither of them noticed.

"I don't want to find out how *not that bad* he is," her mother said. "Okay, Selena? I think he missed his chance to show us how *not that bad* he could be, he hurt me and I'm done with it, a-and I can't lose you too–"

"Mamma I think I let him in."

The clunking grew louder, and something landed hard on the floor. Selena's instrument. Miasmic water washed it forward towards them.

Selena's mother stiffened; her hands dug into Selena as she shoved her daughter behind her and stood up–

"This is for Selena," the clump of water shifted and formed into the warbling shape, the outline of a man. It spoke with vibrating efficiency. "Not for you, Morona. Let her have it back. Or do you not allow her to make her own choices either?"

"Of course she can make her own choices, don't try and convince me that all this is my fault, *you*–"

"Please," the water entoned. "Let's not have a spat in front of Selena. I think she wants to accept my gift."

Selena was staring at the instrument. She crawled forward and took it into her lap. A bit of the water that formed the figure broke off and filled the basin of the instrument, waiting, still.

"H-has it been you the whole time, dad?" Selena whispered.

A strand of water split off and caressed Selena's cheek, absorbing a tear that traced there. "No, unfortunately no, sweet thing," it vibrated. "But I've heard your music, every note. It's beautiful."

The water trembled as Selena Connected to it, pulling one by one the droplets up to strike the strings. A hesitant melody that built atop itself and pulled emotions from the air. Selena shook, but her Connection didn't; all the chaotic jumbles in her mind were rendered notes, and as music she could make them as beautiful as she wanted. All she had to do was make them float.

"You would be happier if your mother couldn't hold you back," the water– her *father*– vibrated. "Listen to the music, you know I'm right."

Selena wept, and her tears joined the melody. "Mamma, I…" But as she looked up to see her mother's face, she just saw agreement. Resigned agreement. It slackened the skin around her mouth, dulled the already dulled light in her eyes. There was knowledge in those eyes.

"Just go," whispered her mamma. "Just go."

"Mamma, I don't want to leave all the time, you just–"

She waved away the protests. "It's fine, Selena. Go. Find out how not bad he is. He's not bad. He's not. He'll treat you well. I'll just… be here."

"I'll miss your laugh, mamma. I'm not going to leave forever. I-I'll come back a-and, check on you, stay sometimes–"

She just shook her head. "Okay, Selena," she said, too drained for tears. "Okay. You don't… yeah. Just go. It's okay for you to go. You should go."

"I'll see you later mamma," the water droplets fell from the instrument as she scooped it into her lap and stood up. "Promise."

"I'm sorry, Morona," the water vibrated as it flowed and seeped to the door. "I wish this all wasn't so hard. Maybe with some time to think on your own, it won't be, and then Selena will want to come back. But of course… this is all up to her."

Selena opened the front door, and together they stepped across the threshold. Instrument clutched tight against her chest, Selena spared another glance back at her mother. She wanted to go to her. To be held one last time. But her mother wasn't looking at her, and in Selena's head the only sounds were the notes of her resentment, playing in such a symphony she felt like they would soon pull her to the stars.

So she stepped outside with her father. She very nearly never looked back. She climbed down, her father swishing back and forth to guide her down the long, long ladder of vines. She stepped onto the forest floor. She watched as all the pieces of her father collected themselves across the floor, dewdrops and puddles slithering through the mud around her.

She couldn't help it though. She looked back up at the house.

*

Selena's mother climbed out of a bedroom window onto the sagging roof of a humble cabin. She didn't worry about her daughter falling from up here, not anymore. After all, her daughter had been up here a thousand times and never fallen. No, what she really worried about was that her daughter would never be able to float away.

She sat on the edge of the roof and thought that her daughter would be better off floating away. Drops of dew glistened like stars on the wide leaves of the canopy, and those little beads of light became all that mother could see. Endless glittering, endless beauty, all of it unreachable. Her daughter could reach it. Reach it and go beyond.

The only thing holding her daughter back... was her. She knew it, and as she came to know it, she slipped forward off the edge of the roof and let herself fall.

Wind. Air. Rushing all around her; a spinning world, and she was full of its beauty, and she was ready, and her only regret which she was rapidly leaving behind was that she couldn't see her daughter one last time, couldn't say goodbye, couldn't even watch her float away–

Something crashed into her, and she was yanked, her momentum stopped. She swung, a firm hand wrapping around her wrist, but it was slipping. She looked up.

Selena. Floating above her, flipped upside down, gripping her wrist, tears in her eyes. "Mamma," she whispered. "Mamma I can't make you float, it's not working, *grab on mamma–*"

She didn't grab on. She slipped further away. "Just go with dad. You deserve better than me–"

"I love you mamma," Selena's voice choked with tears.

"I'm just holding you back. Go. *Float away* Selena, don't let me keep you from floating away–"

"I love you mamma," Selena's grip tightened.

"Have you ever thought that you shouldn't?"

"Yeah mamma all the time– but I love you anyway–" Selena hissed through gritted teeth, her fingers losing color.

Mamma's wrist slipped free, and she fell again. But she saw her daughter's eyes, and all of a sudden she was afraid.

And then she was weightless. She shot upwards, her daughter floating beside her. She could *feel* that raging Connection flowing freely from Selena, linking the two of them, compelling them to rise. They shot up past their house, past the roof. She looked over to Selena, a wild panic in her eyes—but her daughter just smiled and pointed up. The tree branches parted around them, *floating* at a wave of Selena's hand, beckoning them to the world above.

Together, mother and daughter witnessed the cosmos. In times like this one, the stars are so bright even the spaces between them tell stories. The mother pulled her daughter into a hug; as they looked up together, all of infinity reflected in their watery eyes.

"Mamma you need to *talk* to someone."

She squeezed her daughter so tight. "The more I talk to people the harder it is for them to float away," she whispered. "They feel like they can't float away but they *should* because I'm not worth it—"

"I came back mamma, I'm right here—"

"That's the problem, beetroot," she whispered. "I thought for a long time that I was scared of you floating away without me, but I don't think that's true. I think I'm actually scared of you never floating away because you're worried about hurting me, or you feel like you have to take care of me, or that I'm just some weight that always drags you back, a-and maybe—" she felt herself slipping from her daughter's grasp, felt gravity taking hold of her once more.

But Selena was there. "I don't care, mamma. I still love you."

They embraced, and it didn't matter that she was a burden; she floated, there in the space between the stars. They both realized something in that moment. Selena, who had spent all her life imagining the night sky, came to the conclusion that it was even more beautiful than she could ever have imagined. Her mother, who had not imagined the sky in years, came to the conclusion that she should try imagining it more. Both of them agreed however, without exchanging any more words, that the night sky could remain this beautiful for all of eternity, but unlike the world down below the canopy, it could never become *more beautiful*, no matter how much anybody tried. And they both wanted to try, very badly.

So, together, mother and daughter floated gently homewards.

**Joseph Langley** - *Los Angeles, California*
*Hey hey! I'm an aspiring fantasy author based in Los Angeles, California, studying creative writing at Occidental College. I tell stories because they might matter to someone, and because thousands of other people's wonderful stories have mattered to me. Feel free to contact me at joseph.langley888@gmail.com.*

# 7

# *Daniela Călinescu*

## THE FLIGHT OF ICARUS AND THEN PROSECCO

Taking the plane when going on vacation always made me a little fearful of a crash. But it's a mandatory risk in order to land on the promised oasis of relaxation. I would close my eyes or, on the contrary, stare petrified at how the plane rose above the ground, trying to control with my mind the ugly sensation in my stomach.

However, taking the balloon was something else. I didn't have to. Why would I choose to? Again, it was about a choice one can make in order to avoid falling from the sky. The story of Icarus...Why should the desire to enjoy freedom and laugh in the sun be punished by the gods? Why did they let Icarus fall? Why let the parent beg his son to give up joy for the sake of life?

I agreed to fly with the balloon and I dragged my daughter with me. I was scared to death. I imagined there was quite a chance I would not see my husband again, so I left my passport on the table, not telling him the reason. He would figure things out, in case of a tragedy.

It was very early in the morning. The sun was not up yet when we started the journey by car, a 30-minute drive. By the time we got there, the light of dawn was disturbed by the sound of balloons inflating. This is when I saw the size of the basket. It was as if they crowded twelve people in a shopping basket. Most of them were in their late 60s. Was it an ironic gift card that brought them here?

*What are you people thinking?!* I thought in shock.

I took some selfies with my daughter before jumping in the basket – the *before* photos. Then I noted the pilot's youth – he was half my age – and gazed in distrust at the gas installation in his hands. The fire jet disturbed my fragile peace of mind.

Then suddenly, we were floating, light as a cloud. The balloon rose, fellow balloons rose with us, and the rooftops became smaller and smaller. We saw the beautiful colours of the fields, though I couldn't tell if they were 200 or 700 meters away.

Despite the initial fear, I felt so much joy. I was floating above the ground, that terrible fire noise didn't bother me anymore and the gods were not mad at Icarus, he was free.

Soon, we lost height and prepared for landing, but we were still up. I saw a person walking a dog in the middle of the field and I waved energetically with a big smile. He waved back.

Then he waved with the paw of his dog. I couldn't see his face, but I was sure we both shared a good laugh.

At last, we landed, and in that instant of touching the ground I knew I had changed Icarus's story in my mind. I replaced the tragedy with a sentiment of relief.

The organisers gave us a diploma and a glass of prosecco. I drank two.


**Daniela Călinescu** *has been attending the Words of a Feather România workshops since they started in February 2024 in Oradea, Romania, which allowed her to express her reflections on everyday life. She's a 45-year-old mum who enjoys dancing, travelling and exploring visual arts. She has an MA in European Studies from UBC Vancouver and works as a counsellor for European Affairs in public administration.*

# 8

# *Tamara Drazic*

## STARCH

Potato juice dries on my hands, starched linen skin
    left in the sun for three summer days.
Calloused like summer feet, but it's never summer.
I only see you when the heat is expensive.
From the stool in your kitchen,
you watch me grate,
make sure I'm doing it your way.

You exist to me in one-month bursts
every few southern hemisphere summers, skipping time in
between.
We're both older now; there's a chunk missing
when I went from child to adult
and you went from standing in the kitchen
to sitting.

A drop of hot butter burns my hand, but I don't tell you.
We both know we don't have much time left.
You never cry when we leave, but this time
you leak silent tears on my chest.
I wonder what would surface if we were honest.

This time, I know I won't see you again.
But I don't need to tell you.


**Tamara Drazic** *is a writer and librarian based in Melbourne, Victoria. Her work is often inspired by the women in her family, exploring the complexity of cross-cultural relationships.*

# 9

# *Cezar Rozmus*

## FEATHERS DON'T FLY

It was brown. No, beige. No, sepia, no - it was, well... it was just hard to tell. It probably came from a Tawny Frogmouth.

I couldn't care less for feathers. Yet here I was. Captivated. Watching it dance through the air, drifting in slow motion. It was like watching a film frame by frame. As it glided, it brought back the sight of Grandpa waltzing. Never smooth, and yet put him in a pair of dancing shoes, and he would transform instantly. All of a sudden, sliding through the room like a figure skater making love to the ice, reunited at last. Hair immaculate, impenetrable.

Time stood still. That's when every thought crystallised. Suddenly the answer was clear, and right in front of me. This was it. The moment had arrived. *Gulp.*

And yet, I couldn't move. My legs, stiff, begging to be unlocked from their stuck-in-the-mud prison, had statue-d. As my mind raced and explored every possibility, I pondered, could this really happen to me? Would I ever move again? Sometimes, it's better not to know.

My mind instantly inflated with doubts. Like beach balls appearing from beneath the water. These things never just happen. Not to people like me, they don't. No, the universe knew my number and it didn't give a stuff. Never had. Why would I be given a perfect opportunity? Not me. Not now. No way.

The world's quietest breath escaped lips that appeared to be my own. And yet I was stuck. My body was a vessel that contained my mind but had no connection to it. Both were victims of being stuck in a cell with the other. *Why would I want their company?* they asked.

All of the shadows started to descend and became all that I could see. The darkness filled my vision, its own optical illusion, where she simply fell away.

Would I hear her name again? I had never considered myself spiritual, and yet I could feel the universe's clammy breath sticky on my neck. As if she too was watching me to see what would happen next. How should I know?

Had the clouds always been this white? Sending their telegrams to the ocean, telling them what to do with the tides. Or were they too eavesdropping, waiting to enjoy my suffering?

I wanted to say yes, afraid that the loneliness of a no would cripple me for the rest of time. And yet, that word was lodged in my throat. It was like I had swallowed a hair. It wasn't going down and it wasn't coming up. Why do these things happen to me? Couldn't I just, for once, be normal? Probably not.

I just wanted to retract and disappear and evaporate. It was easy. If it was an etch-a-sketch, you'd just turn it upside down, and shake really hard. Then the lines would start to fade. I tried that. Again and again. Nothing happened. This was not an etch-a-sketch.

I just couldn't take it anymore. Was this punishment or was this actually God? Is this why people talk about seeing the light? I couldn't see anything and yet, I could feel all of the entities trying to crowbar their way into my consciousness. Mohammed, Buddha, Lao, all the other ones, the whole lot of them clamouring to solicit advice, or to grab a pew and some popcorn to enjoy the show.

You don't deserve me and I sure don't deserve you. Suddenly, and from nowhere, I inhaled. Where did that come from? Dang, what do I do now? This was supposed to be one of the happiest moments of my life, and I was being eaten alive. My mouth was still ajar.

I froze. I don't know how long for. It was impossible to tell. Maybe the length of one complete disintegration. Who was I? Who was she? A bit of feeling started to come back into my body. Kind of like pins and needles; better than nothing I guess. As if I had been placed in somebody else's body, I started to notice a faint heartbeat somewhere underneath my shirt, or was that an alarm vibrating?

My eyes lifted to reveal the biggest plane I had ever seen gushing overhead. It couldn't have been far above us, and that's when I saw it again in the dusk light. That ruddy feather. But this time, it was light brown, almost caramel, and it floated upwards into the sky to chase the aeroplane. It could have meant anything, and yet I knew exactly what it meant. It was a compass, pointing me to my supposed destination. Feathers don't fly after all, and yet I knew what I was seeing.

"Follow me," she seemed to whisper. I, but an incapacitated devotee, couldn't resist. *Whatever you say*, I thought, or at least witnessed myself think.

"Now open your heart," she murmured.

I'm not a neurosurgeon, but I knew what to do. My body followed orders and inhaled desperately. Then, a deafening exhalation. Was that me? Why did it feel so triumphant? *This is good*, I thought. *Follow the feather*, the compass said. And then it stopped, a bubbling brook.

A plane overhead, a feather talking to me, every doubt I had ever had taunting me, and a sunset slowly dissolving, it was quiet. All sensations still.

Is this it?

And I waited.

And waited.

And waited.

Then, another breath arrived.

"Yes," I heard myself say. "Yes."

**Cezar Rozmus** - *Melbourne, VIC.*
*A passionate storyteller for over two decades, Cezar fell in love with writing at university and has since dabbled in screenplays,*

short stories, and children's tales. Though none are published, the joy of spinning yarns, especially for his kids, keeps his creative fire burning bright, and hopefully theirs, too.

# 10

# *Alexander W.A.J. Bassett*

## DISSOCIATED

Trapped just under my skin
Lost behind my eyes
These hands aren't mine
Left floating around my mind
There's nothing I can do

# FLOATING IN THE IN-BETWEEN

All my nerves are on fire
   It's a sinking feeling,
Dropping me right into the water.
Engulfed in the warmth,
A hug from the water to alleviate the the pain,
Giving me a light feeling.
Whether is rain, shower, tub, pool, river or ocean,
I'm able to drift away.

# YOUR EVERYTHING

Your smile
The way you laugh
Has me trapped in your eyes
If you held my hand, I'd start
Floating

**Alexander W.A.J. Bassett** - *Yarram, VIC*
*Alex is a Writer/Artist from rural Victoria, who enjoys reading and writing horror stories. They are a recently graduated creative writer. Alex runs a writing group in their town, and they volunteer often in their community.*

# 11

## Julie Dickson

## THE GIRL BEFORE

Among the babysitting ads, puppies for sale, and upcoming events advertised on the community noticeboard, I see her face. Marisa. My twin sister. Her green eyes full of wonder and curiosity. The high cheekbones she inherited from Mum, much to my chagrin. Her long wavy, strawberry-blonde hair, so much more appealing than my own dirty blonde. She's wearing her uniform forest green jumper in this picture, taken on school photo day. That's what she was wearing the last time I saw her.

'Here you go, Finley,' says Luke, interrupting my blue funk. He hands me one of the two slushies he's holding. Luke's my best friend. We kissed once to see if there was anything there, but it was too weird, so we stayed just friends.

We leave the 7-Eleven and walk across the cracked concrete to the park and sit at the picnic table under the she-oak tree. It's our after-school ritual.

'So, do you think you'll go to Jessie's party?' he asks. I used to love going to parties but haven't been to one since Marisa disappeared. Dr Whitford says I should start doing the things I did before.

'I don't know, I'm still angry at her.' I stab at my slushie with my straw. 'She took over the role as dance captain only two days after Marisa went missing.'

'Someone had to,' mutters Luke. I glare at him. 'And it's been two months now ...'

'No one in Marisa's dance class thought she'd come back. But Jessie's her best friend. You'd think at least *she* would've held out hope.' I throw my unfinished slushie on the ground, and the lid pops off, spraying pink, icy liquid all over the ground.

*

Luke pulls into his driveway, and I jump over the fence to my house. As I step inside, I'm greeted by a musty odour and a familiar, aching silence.

I run upstairs and push open the door to Marisa's room. It smells unlived-in and still looks like something straight out of a Kmart catalogue—pastel colours and rose golds, tassel bunting on the wall, and fairy lights above her desk and bed. I grab the cloth I keep on her shelf and dust everything, even though I just dusted yesterday. Marisa would freak out if she came home to a dirty room and thought we'd already given up on her.

On her gold wire memo board are her to-do notes. *English essay due Mon 14^th^. Return permission slip for excursion!* They're two months too late. There are also Polaroid photos of Marisa with Jessie and the rest of her dance team. Marisa worked really hard to become the team captain, narrowly beating Jessie. My favourite photo is of me and Marisa at the ice skating rink on our last birthday, hugging and smiling—right before we both fell over. There's also one of us having brunch with Mum and Dad before the divorce. Marisa's lucky she wasn't around to see *that* mess unfold. But, then again, if Marisa had been around, things might've been different.

I glance at my watch. Is it that time already? I run downstairs and jump onto the black leather couch just in time to catch the start of the latest episode of *Lost and Found*, this TV series I watch religiously. It's about missing person cases and how they are solved. I'm on the lookout for tips on how I can bring Marisa home.

I pull out the notebook I keep wedged between the couch cushions. Dad would freak out if he found it. He's a cop, but not assigned to Marisa's case, of course. Most missing person cases are solved within one or two days, but Marisa's case is a cold case because it's been two months, and they still have no leads. That's one of the things I learned from this show.

As the episode comes to an end, I hear the door to the garage roll open and quickly shove my notebook back into its hiding place. Dad's boots plod down the hall, and he appears in the doorway.

'Hey, Finley. Can you heat up some dinner?'

I sigh. No *How was your day, Finley?* I peel myself off the couch and go to the freezer, which is half-full of sympathy meals. The longer Marisa is gone, the smaller the supply becomes. Although, occasionally some of the mums still drop by with a meal because they feel sorry for us.

While the lasagne is heating up, I start to take four sets of cutlery out of the drawer, but my hand hesitates. Sometimes I forget there are only two of us now.

Dad ploughs into his lasagne, while I poke at mine with my fork.

'Your mum's looking forward to seeing you tomorrow,' he says. 'She misses you.'

'Well, if she'd never left, she'd be able to see me every day.'

'Finley,' sighs Dad. 'You know staying here was too hard on her.'

'She's not the only one!'

Dad sighs and rubs his face.

I look at Marisa's empty seat. And then Mum's. I can't believe she did this to us—gave us another empty seat. I stab at my sympathy lasagne.

'Well, I can't see her for long. There's a party I want to go to tomorrow night.'

'A party?'

'It's at Jessie's place.'

'I don't think going to a party is the best thing for you right now.'

'Luke's driving and he's not going to drink and he'll have me home by ten. You know you can trust him.'

'I don't know, Finley.'

'Marisa not being here is hard enough. I can't stop going to parties and doing things.'

'Parties are dangerous, Finley. You—'

'Marisa didn't disappear at a party. And, just because *she* might be dead, that doesn't mean *I* have to stop living my life.'

The room falls silent. I've gone too far. Dad's cutlery clatters on his plate, the sound deafening.

I run upstairs. I can't catch my breath, and my hands are trembling. I see Luke through my bedroom window, sitting on his bed with his sketchbook. He looks up and sees me. *Want me to come over??* he texts.

I shake my head and shut my curtain, collapsing onto my bed and silently crying into my pillow.

The last time I saw Marisa was when we were walking to school one morning last August. We took the shortcut like always—cutting across the footy oval. Marisa said she had to go to the loo and went into the public toilet block. I was distracted on my phone and waited out the front for ten minutes.

I never saw her come out.

I went inside to check on her but couldn't see her anywhere. That's when I noticed the back entrance. But why hadn't I seen anything? Why hadn't I heard anything?

*

Early the next night, Dad's driving me to Mum's place. We haven't spoken much since last night.

I take a deep breath. 'I'm sorry for what I said last night, Dad. I didn't mean it.'

'I'm sorry, too, Finley. It's just that I've already lost Marisa. I can't lose you, too.'

I reach my hand across the console and rest it on top of his, giving it a squeeze. 'You won't lose me, Dad.'

Dad smiles at me. He drops me off at Mum's place, a fancy penthouse apartment in South Yarra.

Marisa's school photo is on display in the middle of a shrine to my missing twin. Two photos of me have been shoved aside.

Mum and I sit at the dining table, eating in silence. Dinner is coconut-crusted chicken with Asian noodle salad. Cooked by her personal chef. I eat slowly, savouring the food that's not a reheated sympathy meal.

'Dad told me you want to go to a party tonight.'

I sigh. 'I'm allowed to have some fun, Mum.'

'Marisa can't go to a party.'

'For all we know, she's run away, changed her identity, and is living it up, going from party to party.'

'You shouldn't joke about that.'

'It's a coping mechanism. If you came to our family therapy sessions, you'd know that.'

'Marisa!'

We both freeze. Realisation dawns in her eyes, and tears threaten. But she's not getting any sympathy from me. Not today.

'Finley, I'm sorry ...'

'I'm leaving.' I push my chair back, scraping the floor.

*

I walk down the street, not wanting to hang around the front of Mum's place in case she comes down. It's dark except for the city lights, and a cool breeze blows. Some girls in their twenties drunkenly wander the streets, giggling and all dressed up for the nightclub. I turn and look behind me and see a figure in the distance. My heart pounds. I walk faster. A glowing 7-Eleven sign beckons. I walk even faster and step into the bright lights of the store. I take a few deep breaths, waiting for my pulse to return to normal, and think about Marisa and how she was taken in broad daylight.

I text Luke to come and pick me up. While I'm waiting, I wander over to the magazine stand and pick up the latest copy of *Girlfriend* magazine and start flipping through it.

Ten minutes later, my phone dings. Luke's here.

'We don't have to go to this party,' he says. 'I can take you straight home.'

'No, let's go. I need a distraction.'

*

The sickly-sweet smell of alcohol hits me as soon as we walk through the front door of Jessie's house. It reminds me of previous parties and how popular I was back then. Music is pounding, and the floorboards are creaking.

As I make my way through the house, everyone turns and stares. Not because they want to be my friend, but because I'm the girl whose sister is missing—presumed dead. My heart races, and my hands are sweaty.

A group of people stop Luke and start talking to him. He gives me a look that says *Sorry*. I shrug. At least everyone still likes *him*.

I spy Jessie at the drinks table filling her cup with punch. I march over, stand beside her, and grab a cup.

'You gave up on Marisa so easily,' I accuse.

Jessie tenses up.

'Two days, Jessie. Just two days.' I slam my hand down, flattening my empty plastic cup. Jessie flinches. 'That's how long you waited before you replaced her. You weren't really her friend.'

Jessie spins to face me. 'I was her *best* friend! I'm the one who encouraged the other girls to choose her as team captain. I was trying to boost her confidence. And then she went missing and we had a competition coming up. *Someone* had to step up as captain.'

'And it just had to be *you*? Maybe you even had something to do with her disappearance.'

'*You* were the last one to see her.'

My chest heaves. I shakily grab the cup from Jessie's hand and tip it on her head. She squeals. I grab the punch bowl and pour the rest of it on her head. Some of it splashes onto me, too, but I don't care.

Someone grabs me by the shoulders and pulls me away. I shut my eyes and scream. Is this how Marisa was taken? But why didn't she scream? Why didn't she call out to me? I was there. I could've helped her. I should've saved her.

The person lets go, and I fall onto a couch. I open my eyes and see Luke kneeling in front of me.

'Fin, it's me, Luke. I'm sorry, okay. I shouldn't have grabbed you like that.'

'Why didn't she scream, Luke? Why didn't I save her?'

'We need to get out of here. Let's talk in the car.'

Luke pulls me up and leads me through the kitchen, out the back door, and to his car.

As soon as I'm inside, I burst into tears. 'I could've saved her, Luke. I could've gone into the toilets with her. But I didn't.'

Luke leans over me and pops open the glovebox. He hands me a tissue. 'You didn't know, Fin. It's not your fault. It's not your fault Marisa disappeared.' He pulls me into a hug, cradling me.

*

When I get home, Dad's sitting on the couch, waiting up for me.

'Your mum called earlier. She told me what happened. You shouldn't talk to her like that.'

'I'm not in the mood, Dad.' I start walking up the stairs.

'Marisa's disappearance has been really hard on her,' he says.

I turn around. 'Mum isn't the only person who has it hard. I have it hard, too. I lost my sister.' I run upstairs and slam my bedroom door.

*

The next day, I'm still curled up in bed at noon. There's a knock on my bedroom door.

'Come in.'

Dad walks in and sits on the edge of my bed. 'Finley, I'm sorry. Your mum and I are on your side, you know, even though we might not act like it sometimes. We're all upset about Marisa's disappearance.'

'Thanks, Dad. I'm sorry.'

Dad pulls me into a hug, cradling me.

*

Later that afternoon, I'm lying on my bed and Luke is sitting near me with his sketchbook in his lap. I scroll through the photos on my phone.

'What should I draw?' asks Luke, tapping his pencil impatiently.

'Draw Marisa.'

'I thought you didn't want everything to be about her.'

'Everything's always going to be about her. It can't *not* be. Draw this photo.' I hold my phone up and show him the photo of me and Marisa hugging at the ice skating rink.

Dad pops his head in. 'Finley, your mum wants you to go over for dinner tonight.'

'But it's not Friday. I only just saw her.'

'She wants to apologise.'

'Only because you spoke to her.'

'Finley, she's really trying to make an effort.'

I sigh. 'Fine, I'll go. But only because I like her food, and I'm sick of sympathy lasagne.'

'Maybe we can start doing some cook-ups together on Sundays? So we have something else to eat?'

I smile. 'Yeah, maybe.'

*

That night, Mum and I eat our dinner in silence, except for the sound of cutlery scraping on the plates. We're eating roast tomato and ricotta pasta. I eat it slowly, savouring the taste.

'You missed the last family therapy session,' I say. 'All of them except the first one, actually.'

Mum sighs. 'I know. I'm sorry. But I've been going to my individual ones.'

'You have?' I ask, surprised.

'I have. The family sessions are too hard for me because seeing you and your father is just another reminder that Marisa is gone. It's really hard for me.'

'It's hard for me, too. She's my twin sister. She was my best friend.' I get teary. 'My sister is gone. And I wanted my mum, but you left. You abandoned me. You—'

'Oh, darling.' Mum leans over and hugs me. She strokes my hair, like she used to do when I was a little girl, and I cry harder. 'I love you, and I'm going to try to be there for you when you need me. I'm working on it.'

I spend the night at Mum's, sleeping with her in her bed, like I used to whenever I had a bad dream when I was a kid. Sometimes Marisa would wake up and join us, so that she wouldn't be alone. I remember now that sometimes Dad wasn't in bed with Mum. Maybe they'd been having problems long before Marisa disappeared.

*

The next afternoon, I wave to Luke through my bedroom window. He smiles and holds up his sketchbook, revealing the finished drawing of me and Marisa. I smile back. It's perfect.

'Finley,' calls Dad. 'You have a visitor.'

I wave goodbye to Luke and run downstairs, stopping when I spot Jessie sitting on the couch. I walk over tentatively and sit across from her.

I take a deep breath. 'I'm sorry about dumping the punch bowl on you.'

'And I'm sorry for what I said.' Jessie fiddles with her skirt. 'Marisa was my best friend. The other girls can't replace her.'

'She was my sister. And my best friend, too. And Luke can't replace her, either.' We share a look. I think I know where she's going with this. Crazily enough, I can see some of myself in her. 'You don't make a very good replacement.'

'Neither do you.'

We smile at each other. I wish Marisa was here to see this.

*

Dad and I are in the car on the way to family therapy. I look out the passenger side window and see another one of Marisa's missing person posters on a bus shelter. Marisa looks back at me, full of hope and wonder and naivety. Maybe that's a good thing because it means people haven't given up on her. But, even when all the posters are gone, I'll still see her face everywhere. As my life moves forward with new relationships and graduation and travel and uni, my heart will still ache for her, but I'll always carry her with me.

*

Dad and I sit next to each other on the couch in the family therapy room. Dr Whitford sits across from us, poised to begin. I stare at Mum's empty spot. The door creaks open, and I look up and see Mum. I smile.

'Am I too late?' she asks.

'Not at all, Angeline,' says Dr Whitford. 'Please take a seat.'

Mum sits down beside me, takes my hand, and squeezes it. Dad squeezes my other hand.

I still hold out hope that Marisa will reappear one day. Because hope is what propels us into the future and gets us through our everyday life.


***Julie Dickson*** *is a writer and editor based in Naarm, VIC. She is the recipient of a Wheeler Centre Hot Desk fellowship, a Varuna Write Space fellowship, and a Writers Victoria Storming the City fellowship. She loves collecting hardcover journals, drinking bubble tea, and using oxford commas.*

# 12

# *Susannah Cosham*

## BROKEN CYCLE

Your mother reads with your four-year-old daughter, wisened finger underlining each word. "Very good," she says whenever Emma pronounces a sentence correctly. They've read this book twenty times. Emma knows it, but your mother's mind is free-floating, unburdened by time or blame.

"I just want you to do your best," she tells Emma, closing the book. It would be a perfect picture—doting grandmother, adored child—if only the simple words were familiar to you too.

This moment could overwrite history. Instead, you feel cheated by how she's made it your duty to heal from the knife that cuts twice.

**Susannah Cosham** *is a writer based in Melbourne, Australia. She has a lifelong fascination with words and stories. She has been creating both original fiction and fan-fiction since childhood, and especially loves crafting tales of exactly 100 words.*

# *13*

# *Brodie Selzer*

## SUSPENSION IN THE INSTANT

Glass-like running water rushed down the busy river, dashing under a thick set metal bridge. At night the moon often glistened against the reflective water, thrashing against the stones that lay beneath and the froth that built up at the river's bank.

Amidst the wind-laced bridges' thick, supporting braces, between the road and sky, a young man shimmied into the corner of two thick metal rods. One leg crossed over the metal, tilting down towards the river, the other towards the road. The night air wasn't nothing, its soft push from the ground became a cacophony of noise at times amidst the iron bridge above the water.

His fingers laced the underside of a brace above his head, as the man searched the incision within it. Unlike the breeze that wafted through the clear sky, his breath held in an impatient clamp within his lungs as his fingers brushed haphazardly within the darkness.

Andrew's frowning lips curled upwards as he stabbed his finger into a small rock hidden within the brace. With rejuvenated effort, despite the lagging, numbing feeling in his arm, he redoubled his search and found the collection of rocks he'd hidden from the sky and wind. He touched the ever-growing spiderweb that hung within the small gap and took the stones out from under the spider's sleeping frame. It had never done anything to hurt him, nor had it thrown the stones away, so Andrew saw no sane reason to rid the bridge of such a fine soul.

Andrew scooped the small rocks out and held them in his open palm as he looked from the river below to the shining road. He paused, reflecting on the humming that echoed through the city at this time of night. He played with the rocks, enjoying the silence that encompassed the bridge. Nothing breathed besides him and the spider, and the bubbling movement of the water beneath them.

He looked on, over the road and through the braces opposite his seat, and out into the open world. The river cascaded under the bridge, into the valley. Andrew could see the large buildings off in the distance, despite a growing mist shrouding the lower city elements from view. The night was growing deeper around the world, like a blanket, its darkness dwarfed by the moon and the brilliant glow of the stars above.

Andrew flicked one of the rocks into the river. His face glowed red as he watched the rock tumble into the clear surface, his breath showing in a gasp of grey clouds. He intentionally shrugged and puffed three more clouds of breath into the night.

Andrew held his breath as he looked about the forest around him. The mountain rose sharply to his right while falling off quickly down towards the valley. The road continued to the top of the white-capped peaks before it dropped into the valleys on the other side.

Andrew brushed his shoulders off consciously, watching small flakes of dandruff waft through the air. His face glowed even brighter, as he pocketed the rocks and ran his fingers through his long, dark brown hair. The slightly curled locks snagged at their tips, knotting from the days it'd been since he'd properly brushed them.

He groaned, inspecting burnt, calloused hands, his centre knuckles wrinkled and hardened by long hours of tossing pans and lifting broken fryer baskets. Andrew sighed inwardly, his lungs expanding past their usual capacity as he stretched the breath as long as possible. When he released, his body sagged, and he drew the remaining rocks from his pocket.

"Thinking of a haircut," he whispered to the valley beneath him. The mountain was completely devoid of audible life, besides his whisper, which carried itself along the passage of water. "Something short, or more... straight?" In truth, he'd had the conversation, this deliberation about so many things many times, and the water reflecting into his dark eyes showed him tonight was another night of questioning.

Trickling water vapour slid down the side of the bridge, running away from Andrew. He leaned backwards into the space above the road, watching the light dance off bright green leaves amidst the forest and leading further down the mountain. Beside the road, a small gap between the foliage and trees stood out like a tiny beacon, the dirt path he'd used to carry himself to the bridge, embracing the kilometres of walking trail rather than simply driving. The trail led a small headway of gaps between the trees, back into the city he called home, such as he could see the trail within the trees from the bridge, through the mass of leaves and softly fallen snow, quickly melting from a storm the day before that had just covered the treetops.

"What am I waiting for?" Andrew asked the wind. Classes, work, art, he'd been working full time on hundreds of projects, but when he climbed the mountain, suspending himself amidst the bridge braces above the river, his mind quietened. He felt a sense of warmth wash over him that had nothing to do with temperature, and his goals became crystal clear, like the moon's brilliant light itself. Andrew frowned and threw three more rocks into the river. He'd have to collect more the next time he climbed.

Preparing to leave the surreal, quiet environment always felt rushed. He spilled both legs over the one side of a brace, dangling momentarily above the river, with nothing to catch him besides a small railing beside the road should he fall.

"Is the river path a burden of fate or a choice of nature?" He wondered aloud, watching the water again. Usually, the water ran smoothly, but tonight it was rough, splashes rocketing up the sides of the riverbank, brushing the underside of the bridge. His expression changed as he dropped onto the road, becoming a mix of a relaxed smile and a comforted sigh.

Andrew flicked his last rock into the river without looking and crossed the road. That was a decision he COULD make, the decision that, at this moment, he was content to walk home, before the snow fell again, and left him freezing in the forest until dawn.

He couldn't see what was standing in front of him tomorrow. Work would be stressful, walking would ease his mind, and the rest of his projects would continue with an ongoing passion of forward momentum. His confidence grew as Andrew descended the mountain, catching his clothes in low-hung branches. Despite that, he smiled the whole way down.

His body may have descended back into the city long before dawn, but his mind sat up in the mountains, where he could safely ponder the next outcome and the forthcoming journey towards it.

He'd carry this feeling, a combination of anticipation, fear, excitement, anxiety, and assertion into his morning; try and carry it through for many days afterwards. This impatient feeling lifted him above any bridge and across any river.


**Brodie Selzer** - *Melbourne, VIC*
*I've been writing since I was 4, next to every day in some capacity. With a notebook in hand, I aim to capture stories within the world and to explore new ones within fiction. I self-published my first novel, Sentinel in 2020, and love going to writing events.*

*14*

# *Eliz Bilal*

## BUTTERFLY LUNGS

The coughing was worse that night. It pricked the back of my throat as I leaned over the bedside table.

*Cough cough cough.*

My eyes began to water

*Cough cough cough*

I felt something emerge on my tongue, small and feathery. With my index finger and thumb, I plucked it out of my mouth. A monarch butterfly. Its small rusty brown and black wings were wet and weak, while its small legs twitched ever so slightly until they stopped and it lay lifeless in the palm of my hand. My hands cupped its small frame. I sat there unable to lift my body up to flush it down the toilet, throw it in the bin, or out the window for the birds to eat. I could not bring myself to do it.

The morning light crept through the curtains. The digital clock which sat on a stack of an Emily Bronte book collection flashed *6:00am*. A tear pricked my eye as I stared at the fragile creature. It was my fault. I had killed it. I could not keep it alive. I stood slowly from the bed, my feet sunk into the fluffy rug and out emerged Calliope, a stray cat I had found on my window seal two years ago. She would often knock her tiny white paw on the glass, knowing there was food waiting for her from behind the screen. Where she came from always remained a mystery, but we found each other. Her green eyes widened but I ignored her request for breakfast. By the window, a monstera plant sat, its large green leaves arched in all different directions. I nestled the butterfly next to a small leaf. With the back of my hand, I wiped the tears across my cheek, lifted Calliope, and nuzzled her furry white head into the crook of my shoulder. She purred softly against me. Until I felt another prick in the back of my throat.

**Eliz Bilal** - *Melbourne, VIC*

*Hello! My name is Eliz Bilal and I am a writer from Naarm. I love writing stories that incorporate magical realism with a gothic twist.* Butterfly Lungs *is a small extract from a novella I am currently writing, titled* A Room Full of Butterflies. *It is a tale about a girl in her mid-twenties named Niya whose world begins to fall apart but will ultimately transform her. This extract gives a small taste of what to expect in this magical yet unnerving tale.*

# 15

## *Kartiya Ilardo*

### YOU

Cosiness is
    warm flesh
at around 9pm
tied around your waist
interlaced

cosiness
is the allure when we
stand on opposite sides of
the room

cosiness is
being held by
eyes exactly like mine
but you haven't that noticed yet

cosiness
is the dull sweetness
of mint as your breath
hugs my tongue
and dances in my chest

cosiness is
watching you talk
and seeing flashes
of little you
pass by your face

cosiness
is those moments
of desire
where it's over
and you're like sand
falling through our
kissing palms
and that lingering...
the drag away from
your gaze
I tear myself
and it feels cold again
don't you feel it
too?

**Kartiya Ilardo** - *Melbourne, VIC*

*Kartiya is the co-founder of The Provocative Inklings. She graduated The University of Melbourne with a Bachelor of Arts in Psychology and Creative Writing, and has recently earned her Masters in Teaching Early Childhood and Primary. Her passion is to create, whether it be through words, film or dance. It is through these she feels most alive and where she can appreciate the beautiful gift that is life. Find her work on her Instagram: @kartiya.ilardo*

# 16

# *E.I.Tera*

## REDDISH PUDDLE

*content warning: language, violence*

Sometimes I think about ending it.

Put an end to all the suffering. The bruises heal and the scabs fall. But who can give me a new psyche? One that doesn't tell me I deserve what's happening?

Is it true that if Otto doesn't want me, no one else will?

At first he wasn't like that. He was attentive and caring. He would open the door and take me by the arm as we walked into the moonlight. He would buy me flowers and write me love letters.

Like a wolf in sheep's clothing, he bared his fangs after I moved in with him.

Maybe I was too messy or didn't hold on to money the way he wanted me to. It started gradually. I'll never forget the first slap, the first cigarette butt burn. I'm a living wound, and every scar tells a story.

The last time we quarreled, he poured boiling water on my palm. The pain didn't go away until the next day. The argument started over the way I dress. Apparently, my summer clothes are far too revealing.

I'm tired of thinking that whatever happens is my fault.

I'm thinking about putting a stop to it. For the first time, I'm actually going to take action.

I'm going to do it no matter how lonely I feel afterwards, even if I end up on the streets and no one wants me anymore.

It's hard to end a relationship with a stubborn person who can't see they're wrong. But it's much harder to research the most effective ways to end their life. The internet's playing dumb, not telling me anything.

I wanted to smother Otto in his sleep, but from what I saw in a murder documentary, it's harder than it looks. What if I couldn't do it, and he would kill me instead?

I often thought about pushing him in front of a car as we waited to cross the street. The whole thing would have looked like an accident. But on second thought, it's not sure that would kill him either.

I finally chose what made the most sense. Rat poison. A few drops in his coffee, a few in his water bottle, just a pinch in the curry paste. I didn't know if that would really be the end of it. But it was worth a try.

Today, on what I hope will be Otto's last day, the poison kicked in. All day he's been in the bathroom, the sound of vomiting echoing through the apartment.

I had hoped it would work, yet Otto wasn't as stupid as I thought. He knew I'd done something to him.

"Listen here, you cheating whore. You're a–"

Before he could finish, another wave of vomit caught him off guard. This one showed traces of cucumber and the smell was unbearable. For the first time, I'm not a servant ant, willing to clean up immediately.

Furious, he curses. He grasps his stomach, drained of strength. But even that can't keep him from acting on his rage. He throws the vase of wilted flowers at my head. It breaks. Blood, lots of it.

"I don't know what you did to me, but you'll pay for this!"

From there, it's a full-blown fight. He hits me in my stomach, in my tits, in my face, everywhere. He slams my head against the wall. He makes sure to curse me all the while. At one point the pain seems numb. *Will I die here, next to him? Is this my end?* I wonder.

I lie in a pool of blood. Otto collapsed long ago. I'm floating. Floating to a new life. There, this blood will turn into water. Water means life. I'll be better, happier. My plan worked.

If now I float in this reddish puddle, tomorrow I'll float in one of hope.

Despite my numb limbs, I rise. Time to clean up…

**E.I. Tera** *is a creative writer based in Oradea, Romania. At the moment, she's studying for a Bachelor's degree in Journalism. She usually writes non-fiction pieces, as well as long and short-form fiction.*

## 17

# *Pluto Cotter*

## SPINNING MIND TO HEAD SPINS

The sheets crinkle beneath me, sage green and soft. I lug the king-sized doona over the top of me in the stolen bed I call my own. The clothes piled in front of the open closet call my name, begging to be put away. I feel the eyes of the images stuck to the wall behind me judging me for the mess strewn on the carpeted floor. My friends glare down wondering who I've become. My family pleads with me, longing for me to change.

The mess has begun to migrate; up onto the chair, bedside table, and set of shelves. The vapes strewn across the bedside table are dead now, all that remains is a trickle of liquid and the taste of a burnt coil. I'll bring it to my lips anyway, thinking I should open the giant blind next to my bed and unscrew the window, push it open and re-secure it.

I shouldn't rot in a mess that smells like sweat and vape, but I don't think I care.

The books on the shelves scream to be read, they deserve it, but where can I muster the energy from? I have changed too much now to be bothered snatching one up and being devoured by its words.

The vape taste clings to my tongue, sticky and disgusting. It makes my throat burn with this taste of burnt wood. I swap it for another that tastes slightly sweeter but still leaves the same taste of singed tree. There will be a fire in my lungs, I think. On the day sucking on a green battery catches up to me. It did taste good, for a while, back when the flavours of Grape Peach Ice still existed within its cartridge. The economy, however, didn't spare me in its capitalism crusade and I have now fallen to limited spending.

I did buy a pack of smokes today, sometimes they sooth the thirst for nicotine better than a vape. Well, I didn't really buy a full pack. I gave my girlfriend $15 to split half a 20 pack of Blue Classics (she too has fell to the face of university poverty.) They helped to soothe the desperation to place the burnt battery back in my mouth. I crave it always.

So, I sit in my bed filling my lungs with smoke that has chemicals I can't even begin to name, hoping it may make the spinning of my mind stop. I stare at the collection of off-brand Lego dinosaurs that sit on the shelf at the end of my bed. I wanted to collect more but now I'm unsure if there is a reason to it. Is there much reason to anything? I don't mean to be nihilistic, but when the bank runs dry, the classes feel stressful, and the job hunt is an endless stream of rejection, what is the point of doing anything?

I suppose that's too much to question as the burnt vape juice stops my mind from spinning and the head spins begin. I worry it'll make me nic sick, but I won't let that stop me as I take another puff. The smell permeates my room again and I feel trapped in the cocoon that is my bedroom.


**Pluto Cotter** *- Melbourne/Naarm, VIC*
*I am a Melbourne University student from the far off lands of Far North Queensland, working hard to not be so consumed by first-year studies that I lose all passion to create.*

# 18

## Livia Creț

### REVERIE

A seasonal endeavor: straightening up our homes.

The spring-cleaning frenzy is in full bloom; people become self-conscious about the piling dust in the corners and on the upper shelves. I remember how my mother would panic during this time, which happened to be a few weeks before Easter; she'd think she was running out of time, and that she could not finish all the tasks by the arrival of presumed guests who never crossed our cleaned threshold.

A common feature in my family, in my culture really, is that spring bears stress. My mother would happily clean the house, trim the courtyard, remove the weeds from the garden, sweep, wash, etcetera, only if it didn't involve time because time is, in fact, the enemy, not the muddy floors or dusty trinkets, or the flowers waiting to be tented.

I've crossed four borders to Aulnay-sous-Bois to have the farcical revelation that this quarrel with time is a natural tendency in humans, that stretches beyond the perimeters of my country.

I hear my neighbor downstairs knocking over furniture, moving dressers, refashioning the house for a few hours every day (in the past week), trying to wipe the place clean, to the last window rim, fridge handle, and electric switch.

The spring-cleaning frenzy attacks from ground level and mounts menacingly upstairs, where it creeps into my sitting-room and subjugates my sponge-like receptive mind. It is in this soaking state of readiness that I follow in the footsteps of my mother.

I take out the broom – *swuushh*

                         move the couch — *Wuushhh*

                             lift the shoe rack – *Ushhh-hhsss*

    sweep the lamp holder

        the corners

        the hardly accessible joints

        the threshold

                   switch to mopping

                      mop the fake wooden floor

                         and the cracked bathroom tiles

         *'you've finished with the mop*
*then you can stop*
           *and look at what you've done'*
  the floor is speckless, the house is clean except
           I still have to defrost the fridge
         wipe it clean
         wipe the windows till they
shine in the spring sun
         wash the bedsheets
         the cupboards
         put my tea collection in order
of preference
         sort my notebooks in a pyra-
midal shape
   the bottom—not using them again
   the top—priority boarding for school trips
         remove spider webs (not the
spiders, those I'm scared of)
  god, it's good I don't have rugs, I can't wash rugs and don't
have the strength to carry them to the cleaners
  I take it upon myself to make sense of the design incon-
sistencies and the architectural deficiency of my building and
thus make this household pleasant enough to survive in until
  now
  sift and sort through the futile objects gathered in the past
months like the most severe editor would
  dust off the kitchen appliances
  (possibly make myself a black tea to boost my cleaning
spree)

put every plate and pot in its place
and finally
job done
house clean
inherited stress disorder carried forward
now
take the trash out and
     yourself on a city date.


                        hop on
  Platform littered, people grumpy, I        the train and
swiftly search for a seat,

found it!

RER B

*Blanc-Mesnil*
black suit, black socks
probably black underwear,
and black shoes. They think
they shield themselves, but their life
is transparent through the
scissors cufflinks and pin.
Did they want to become a *coiffeur*
but end up a *corporatist* instead?
'Sarah... on l'entend pas souvent'
*Drancy*
                        short curly hair

powder pink mask
cheetah print fur
short checkered skirt
a notebook in hand
they underline words

'Ouai, c'est à l'origine anglaise j'pense'
*Le Bourget*
a bald circle at the top
of their head and deep
wrinkles making it
look like a dried potato
forgotten at the bottom of the bag
'Mais toi, t'as des origines espagnoles, c'est ça?'

*La Courneuve-Aubervilliers*
tall, blonde hair
Marshall headphones
reading Phillip K. Dick
can't figure out the title
there are several cramped
bodies between us

'Bah non, du côté de mon père j'suis allemand'
*La Plaine-Stade de France*
they get down chanting
singing *Delilah* on
their way to the rugby game
'On a tous des trucs allemands…'

*Gare du Nord*
vampiric outfit
white shirt, long puffy sleeves

black coat, black curls
long nails, circular piercings
ruby necklace

They stop talking and prepare to get off at
*Châtelet-les-Halles*

When I get off the train I stop for a moment and marvel at this girl's carrot orange eyelashes. It wrecks me for an instant and I feel stranded from the crowds heaping at the car doors, isolated in the distance from my eyes to her eyelashes—so rare—of another color than organic black.

I wake up from my reverie and find my way to
Metro 11

*Rambuteau:* a man on the opposite platform carrying a wooden board that looks very much like a door? And his being there marks the intention to get on the metro WITH said door.

*Arts et Métiers* is painted in bronze and looks like the inside of a submarine.

*République* is plain: white tiles and movie posters.

*Goncourt:* named after the writer brothers after which the literary prize is named.

*Belleville:* green seats and cheese advertisements.

Next one is mine:          *Pyrénées* like the mountains.

Here I am with my foot on rue de Belleville: roasted chicken stands, cuisine *anatolienne, grecque...*

Painted on a building:  LA NUIT, MON CORRI-
DOR.

     I take
a left
    walk
        the
    curving
road
train my eyes on a brick apartment building: on each side
of the six-bathroom windows the paint peels off, larger por-
tions on the upper floors narrowing to the size of streams,
then tears.

Why are they named *villas*, these narrow cobblestone
streets with gates taken over by roses and cats? I stare into peo-
ple's courtyards, violating the intimacy of their home deco-
rations: young trees in pots, DIY bird houses, weathercocks,
printed dumpsters, Japanese poems on paper plates and ironic
entrance signs: *En cas d'absence, je ne suis pas là. Si vous n'êtes
pas là non plus, il n'y a donc personne.*

        I walk uphill on Villa de Belleville
         arrive at rue de Belleville

  take a
left

        end up at campus Bellevue
        where there is a food stall

                        in the shape of a 60's Volkswagen
van,

                        white and green.

Many turns have led me to:
                *Il faut se méfier des mots*

Inside *Culture Rapide*:
                I Chose The Road
                Less Traveled.
                Now, Where The
                Hell Am I?

What does *fast culture* mean in a world
where we rely on pictures to remember
of fast-paced environments
*trains de grande vitesse*
and YouTube shorts?
How do all these tie together
and contribute to the brief and worrisome
attention span           what can you fit in 47 seconds?
of today's population?

*__Livia Creț__ is a creative writer based in Romania, juggling short stories and creative nonfiction pieces. She received her MFA in Creative Writing from the University of Kent in 2023. In partnership with Amy Han, the founder of the creative writing studio Words of a Feather, she opened a Romanian* branch of the studio in her hometown, Oradea. Her works of fiction and poetry have appeared in Romanian and English literary magazines, both in print and online.

# 19

# *Amy Han*

## UNDER A STARLESS SKY

I'm 23 years old, carrying £3000 cash in an envelope tucked into my coat pocket. It's 2.30 am. Beanie on and hood over my head, walking quickly down Fulham Broadway back to the shared apartment by the river Thames. On the weekends, my flatmates and I walk along the bank and watch the posh families watch their teenage children race boats. I always think it would be fun to be the person with the megaphone, facing back towards the team, calling *stroke, stroke, stroke,* while getting a ride along the water on a Saturday morning. It feels like another time and place, those weekends, while I speed walk under streetlamps, head down, hands in pockets, pretending.

I work at a little Chinese restaurant on the border of Fulham and Chelsea. It's owned by a young couple from Hong Kong. Michelle runs the business while Geoff, her husband, works as head chef. In the kitchen downstairs, there are huge white buckets full of chicken floating in cornstarch water. The freezers are full of every dumpling you can imagine. Michelle reminds me that we are far from Chinatown here: none of the customers are Chinese, the British people don't know how to use chopsticks, and when they order a whole fish, I must fillet it away from the table, because they don't like to see the head.

The assistant chef's name is Nelson. He's almost 30 but looks 15. He's here from Malaysia on a student visa. On one of my first days, Michelle asks me to help him with his visa paperwork because my English is good.

"What do you study?" I ask him.

Nelson chuckles at the table beside me. "Oh, I no study, Amy. Geoff just help me with my visa. I pay money and I work here. Stamp, stamp," he says, making a stamping gesture over the forms.

I've never been a waitress before. I was meant to find a job in book publishing. London – the home of some of the greatest writers who ever lived, a well-established and respected hive of bookish creation and activity – was the perfect city to gain that experience. But the year is 2008 and the whole world is falling apart. There are no jobs, not for a young Australian fresh out of uni, with no professional experience, on a working holiday visa. Locals were more depressed than usual, apparently, and the tube trains were often held up due to another fatality on the tracks.

So here I am. I work for free for literary agents and children's book publishers, paid in the honour of being there and occasionally lunch and travel money. The rest of the time, I'm in this restaurant, paying my rent by serving Chelsea football supporters with a smile. I teach them how to use chopsticks and recommend the house wine I've never tried. I ignore flirtatious remarks because when I smile they stay longer, buy more beer, and leave me a bigger tip at the end of the night.

Michelle is so delighted to have a native English speaker on the team that she promotes me to head waitress two weeks after I start. I feel bad because the other waitresses have been here longer, but we get along well and they seem happy not to have the extra responsibility. I work mostly with Pana, who is from Thailand and has a face like a doll. She crinkles her brow at the wasted food that comes back. When Michelle isn't looking, she squats behind the bar and pushes crispy, untouched spring rolls through her glossy pink lips.

"We're going back to Hong Kong," Michelle announces to me one afternoon. "We'll be gone for three weeks. You're in charge. Nelson will take care of the kitchen. All I need you to do is clear the register each night. Can you do that? Just put the money in an envelope with the report, take it home, and I'll collect it all when I'm back."

*

On the first Saturday night, boss-less, the last customers put their coats on and leave just before midnight. Pana and I clear and wipe the tables, and set them all again for tomorrow. She's vacuuming the carpet and I'm drying glasses when Nelson pops his head up the stairs.

"Finished?" he asks.

"Yeah, just cleaning up."

"Oh. You like dumpling?"

"Huh?"

"Dumpling. You know? Dim sum?"

"Yeah! Of course."

"I make for us. Yeah?" he looks between us, like he's asking for permission.

Pana nods enthusiastically, her face lighting up for the first time all night. "Yes, yes!"

So here we are, the three of us – Nelson from Malaysia, Pana from Thailand, and me from Australia – in a suburban London Chinese restaurant, seated at a round table with a basket of every possible dumpling spread across the lazy Susan. We sip tea and rotate the baskets between us, talking about everything, until the dumplings are all gone and we've run out of words, sleepy.

"That was amazing," I say.

Nelson nods. "I make but I never eat. Only one time, when I first start."

"Thank you," I tell him.

"Don't tell Geoff." He smiles, holding a finger over his lips.

I clear the register. We turn off the lights, lock the door, and walk our separate ways. The cold November air stings my nose and burns my cheeks. There's a bus that could take me home and sometimes I think that would be smarter. *Things happen to young women alone at night* is always a sentence floating around the periphery of my mind. But I feel the need to walk. I insist on prioritising this need over doing what I'm told, even with the floating *I told you so*'s drifting through me, hovering over my dead body in the version(s) of my life in which I should have chosen the bus, shouldn't have taken a job that finished late, shouldn't have moved to London, should have stayed home, should have dressed differently, shouldn't have been wearing headphones, should have smiled more.

I need to walk to walk off the banter, the ache of smiling and pretending to find things funny that I don't, the glasses that crack in my hands under too-hot water, and the other hands that have brushed past my skirt.

I need to walk off the privilege of choosing to be here, 'for the experience', when I could go home and find a more stable job that utilised my university degrees. I need to not think about the divide between Nelson and Pana and I, even though this moment in time has brought us together.

*

There is a section of the high street that is crowded with pubs. On a Saturday night, at 2.30am, most of them have closed but the drunkest of the men are still out – the ones who lost track of time and missed the last train, and will eventually have to call a black cab home.

"Ey, sweetheart," one of them calls out to me as I pass.

I clutch the envelope in my pocket and pretend not to hear him, walking faster.

"Ey! Ey, you're not deaf, are you? She's a deaf bird."

"Prolly doesn't speak English, mate," another one says.

*"Ni hao? Ni hao?"*

*"Konichiwa?"*

They burst out laughing.

I feel them stumbling behind me.

"Ey, ey, slow down."

"Leave 'er alone, mate."

"I just wanna talk."

"Ey."

There's a hand on my arm and in one version of my life I whip around and slap his pink, white face. In that version of life, I push his drunken block of a body over. He's heavy and one of his friends breaks his fall. In one version of that life, they laugh, rolling over on the frosty concrete. In another, the first guy gets up and lunges for me. I duck away, or I push him again, or he grabs me and pushes me up against a wall. His friends pull him off, or they hold me down. The envelope slides out of my pocket; one of them opens it, and takes it. It's me on the frosty concrete, alone, with empty pockets, and no way to prove that I didn't simply keep the money for myself. Sometimes I scream but it doesn't make a difference. Sometimes there's another person nearby who helps. In one version, a police car just happens to be rolling past. In several versions of my life, I end up dead.

I pretend not to feel the hand on my arm and keep on walking. The envelope is a broken wing in my fist. He doesn't grab me. "Leave 'er, mate, leave her," one of his friends calls. He doesn't follow me, but the part of my arm he touched seeps through my layers into my skin. It bleeds down to my fingers, up into my shoulders; it sets my whole body on fire.

*I told you so, I told you so.* My face is wet, and I'm running. I'm puffing frosty clouds, running with my hands in my pockets, crushing the envelope packed with cash. I keep running towards the river, glistening in the moonlight. I run and run under a starless sky.


**Amy Han** *is a writer and the founder of Words of a Feather, a studio for young* writers of all ages. She writes mostly novels for younger readers, and short stories and personal essays for older readers. Having said that, she simply writes, without really wanting to put a label on any of it. You can find more of her writing at: amyhan.com.au*

# 20

# *John Chen Tze Jet*

## WORKING THROUGH PAIN

Staying functional is a matter of taking step after step, breath after breath.

I've been finding victories in the littlest things: cooking my own meals, texting back a friend, tidying my space. They are just the smallest things, but keeping a full fridge, dusting off the old piano, or dressing better before heading out, are all reasons to celebrate. Some days, I find that success isn't so much in making leaps of progress. Some days, it's simply winning the fight not to regress.

Some days, I might not win that fight. Some days, I might cry, and some nights, I might drink. I might kick and I might scream, and on worse days, I admit I might morbidly wonder just how quickly a tram could crush the human body, and on worse nights I might have simply wished to silently slip away in my sleep. But, those thoughts exhaust the mind into numbness eventually. Then, I'll stand at the bathroom mirror and be met with a familiar man, now with unkempt hair, poor skin, bags under tired eyes, and alcohol on his breath. I'll face him to tell him once again, "There is more to life."

I'll tell him there is more to life. And he might struggle for a moment to believe it. But he'll come around. He always comes around. He survives and, at least for the night, no more indulges the anxious, the vicious, the unloving voices. He *does* listen to the quiet voice in the back that tells him, "This is worth it." For what or for whom, exactly? He doesn't really know — yet somehow, he believes it.

So, he stays alive another day, to take another step and to take another breath.


**John Chen Tze Jet** - *Melbourne, VIC*
*Just a guy who thinks too many thoughts, feels too many feelings, and likes to magnify the little things in life. Occasionally, he puts pen to paper to get the words out and to try and make sense of it all.*

# 21

# *Aaron Agostini*

## INSURANCE POLICY

My head
        runs a house on fire
so it becomes of me
to put it out.
watch me douse myself
in liquor
until I sit on the edge of my roof,
hoping
and praying
that
on the ground below me
there will be
a fireman
who will
catch me

when I finally decide
it's time
to come down.

# LUNATIC

I found myself
  at
the edge of night
and
between phases
that
in retrospect
seem to be just another cycle I run through,
and
all I could think about
before
I fell asleep
was
how weird it is
that
every time we seem to be headed toward the light at the
end of the tunnel
  we are also headed
in the opposite direction
of
someone we love.

# I'VE BEEN LIVING LIKE A RACECAR

With only 4 wheels,
     and
I've been lying like a riverbed
slowly growing shallow,
and
I've been weeping like a rug
stuck to a humid sticky floor,
and
all I've been thinking about
is
this fear of being loved
and
the lengths I would go
to
leave it on the side of a highway
and
drive away in some kind of vessel
that
could actually make it some impressive distance
before inevitably breaking down
again.

**Aaron Agostini** *(Melbourne, Australia) is a scientist from New Jersey who cannot drive, but totally could if he really wanted to. His website is: aaronagostini.com*

# 22

# Elias Hart

## THE BIRDS

*content warning: blood, violence, implicit allusion to suicidality*

The first time Matthew picked up a camera was when he was fifteen. The first picture he ever took was of me standing in front of a dilapidated building, my skinny frame draped in a black leather jacket I stole from the thrift. We grew up together, Matthew and I: me and my loud, echoing laughter and him, with his head of tousled black hair that back then, almost touched his lashes which he would re-flexively brush away from his eyes. Back then, he always looked at the ground even when people were talking to him or at a faraway place that floated in the distance, like some sort of white light that only he could see.

The only times he ever did look straight ahead was when he had a camera in his hand. His voice, which was soft and sometimes barely audible, would snap into sharp instruction as he motioned at his subject to stand in a particular manner. His fingers, which usually trembled, held the camera, cool and controlled. And his photos inspired a sense of wonder in me; I admired how beautiful he made his subjects look, which in turn made me sad, because whenever I tried to take a photo of him, he ducked out of the frame and shielded his face on instinct.

When he started photography, I was his muse-subject, mostly because we were together every day and because we didn't have many friends. My favourite portrait he took of me was of my jet-black hair pinned straight to my shoulders. My skin was a cold, marble white. I was wearing nothing but the leather jacket. I usually hated pictures of my body, which once, a boy had exclaimed looked so much like a man (huge bulking shoulders), I retreated home, angry and humiliated, and dove straight into Matthew's arms, pressing my breasts into his chest, peony cheek against his and kissed him on the mouth. To my surprise, he returned my kiss and this went on for hours until we lay breathless, lying on our backs, staring at the ceiling above. Afterwards, he caressed my hair with his pale white fingers, telling me how beautiful I was.

It was my first and last time with Matthew, because before long, he started dating this banker named Lucien.

"Why did you kiss me back then?" I asked him, late at night, the candle flickering in the gloom.

"You looked so sad. I thought it would comfort you."

It was such a serious, straightforward answer. I had laughed and watched his face grow puzzled at my amusement.

*

What drew me to Matthew was this exact seriousness—this obligation to responsibility. He possessed this astute ability to sense suffering and soothe accordingly.

When we lived in an apartment together during university, he would crawl out of his bed quietly in the morning to gaze at the white birds that swooped down onto the pavement. He took a photo of these birds which resembled a pool of white pebbles that streaked through the air and landed in perfect circles on the ground. He took a photo every day for three months. Occasionally, there would be a bird, a little smaller, a little frailer than the rest, with a broken wing or a swollen eye, or walked with a limp. Each time they appeared, Matthew would go downstairs, cradle it in his arms, and carry them to our apartment, hoping to nurse the bird back to health. In the daytime, he carried the crippled bird like a child in his arms to the vet and returned home with medicine and bird supplies. And in the nighttime, he prayed for their health. When the birds grew stronger, he opened the window and released them into the air. We stared at the arch of its pearl white wings soaring through the sky. It was times like this that made me love him so much.

"The Florence Nightingale of wounded birds," I said to him. He blushed shyly.

Sometimes I wondered why he took photos every day. It was a peculiarity, sure, but I never thought it strange or out of place as someone might have, considering Matthew never suggested he would make a career out of photography. It was something he enjoyed— a simplicity he relished in. At least that was what I initially thought. We were both quiet people, preferring to read and paint in silence than indulge in conversation.

Sometimes, he would remain quiet for days. He was somewhere I could never reach. When he entered these periods of melancholy, the hours grew longer and bleaker. When these periods stretched out for weeks, I grew resentful at his silence which I interpreted as avoidance. Had I done something to upset him? This unpredictability disturbed me, but I swallowed my rage and confusion and instead tried my best to wait patiently for him to return to me.

But finally, when he was in one of his livelier and more talkative moods, I decided to ask him about the birds.

"Why do you take photos of them every day? You must have hundreds by now." The sky was hazy, casting light that made the mornings feel distinctly dreamy and unreal. He was leaning out the window, his pale fingers wrapped around a cup of tea.

"Promise you won't laugh, Elaine."

"Of course I won't. Why would I?"

He blushed. "Well, Lucien did when I told him. He said that I am simply wasting time taking photos that I'd never sell."

Of course he did. I never quite liked Lucien, who seemed listless when they were together, like he was always out of time and needing to return to the office.

"Well, Lucien's practicality limits his imagination."

This made Matthew smile, and then he spoke.

"In the beginning, I thought the birds looked beautiful. Like little white angels. They contrasted well against the industrial landscape. So, I wanted to document that. But the more I did, the more attached I became to it."

"To the birds?"

"No, not the birds. The birds were a side-effect. I was attached to the act of photographing them. It became part of my routine like having a meal. I wouldn't know a day without it. The very act is like a compass, something that anchors time to a still. It reminds me that I'm still here," he gestured around the apartment. "That I'm still here on this day, with you." He turned to me and smiled wryly as a strand of black hair blew loose and curled around his temple. I wanted to reach out and tuck it behind his ear until suddenly, he flushed red, like he had realised he revealed something he shouldn't have.

I paused a few moments for reflection and then asked.

"And the sick birds? How can you tell that they are in need of help? Is it how they walk?"

"Partly. Most of the time, I notice the birds who seem removed from the rest. They're not ostracised but it's clear to me that they've willingly isolated themselves. So usually, they're alone, several meters away from the centre of the action, trying to blend in. But their desperation to imitate further alienates them."

I turned to face him but he was staring in the distance again like he did when he was a boy. His gaze was austere, but his large eyes and fluttering eyelashes were so childlike. He had retreated within himself, escaping into his own mind, and I expected that the rest of the day would be veiled in silence.

*

One morning, Matthew and I were making breakfast. I was spreading butter on a piece of toast and he was waiting for the water to boil in the kettle, staring out the window, when suddenly he let out a scream. I turned to him in alarm until I saw that a bird was flying at full velocity at our window—a window that was shut closed. But neither of us could do anything before we heard the piercing thud, as the bird slammed into the glass, and collapsed to the pavement below, leaving a streak of blood smeared on the windowpane.

It was Matthew that acted first. He ran downstairs as I stared at the bloody streak.

By noon, Matthew returned upstairs and said he had buried the bird. We didn't speak for the whole day.

*

One evening, I was alone in the apartment, anxious and waiting for Matthew to return from class. The electricity had gone out and I had candles flickering in the otherwise dark rooms.

It was nine at night and his class finished at four. I was pacing around the kitchen, counting and glancing surreptitiously at my watch, thinking whether to call Lucien's bank, or barge into the police office, when the door flew open, followed by hurried footsteps, and then there Matthew was— black hair in disarray, eyes crazed, standing in complete silence.

"Matthew— what's wrong. Why are you home so late?" I snapped and immediately regretted it.

That was when I noticed he was clenching his fist, and he was shaking—not just his hands—but his whole body. I went cold and took a tentative step forward.

"Matthew, what happened?" I placed a hand on his arm, and he flinched. He stepped back on reflex, knocking into the table with the flickering candle, as I cried out and leaped forward to catch his fall. With my arms interlocked around his waist, fingers almost digging into his ribs, I realised that he was not wearing the jacket he left the house with. And when I withdrew my hands from him, my palms came out smeared with something warm and liquid. My eyes met his and as the candlelight shone on his body, I finally noticed that half his shirt was soiled with blood.

"What happened, Matthew?" My voice rose in panic. He was staring at me with that look of dread and fear and something else.

"Elaine, I was walking home. I was and someone, I think he was following me and I don't know, I don't know but he took my things." Matthew shook his head nervously. "He took my wallet, Elaine. And my camera. Everything. He took everything." He had that frantic, delirious look in his eyes that scared me. And he was limping now, trying to pace around the kitchen.

"Matthew, you're hurt. You need to lie down." I tried to sound authoritative. I tried to sound like Lucien. *What would Lucien do right now?*

"No, I can't, Elaine. I just can't," he said, completely broken and exasperated. "He took my camera, Elaine."

"You need to lie down, Matthew." My voice rose into a shout which frightened him like I knew it would. Usually, that was all it took to get him to calm down. But this time something had changed.

He winced, recoiled, and walked backwards as I strode forwards, pleading with him to calm down, to let me see his wounds. But the more I spoke, the more frightened he became. This made me fearful and overcome with guilt which accelerated to irritation and finally anger. I clutched his shoulders, stared into his eyes (eyes that seemed like open wounds) and hit him across the cheek.

He went still like a dead animal. Even his shaking stopped.

I wanted to cry, but instead, I rolled up my sleeves and methodically removed his shirt, resisting the urge to vomit, as I stared at a burgeoning red gash searing his white flesh. He had gone inert, and I fetched the first aid kit, bandaging him up in despair. When I was done, I tried to lift him to the bed but he was too heavy. Finally, in exhaustion, I wrapped him in a blanket and left him slumped against the wall, as I rushed into my bedroom, silently crying and dialling Lucien's number in desperation.

I somehow convinced Lucien to let Matthew live with him for a while. Lucien lived in a better part of town where the air and view, I said, would be restorative to ill health. Of course, this was only partly the truth. I also couldn't bear to face Matthew, who grew more distant as the days dragged on. I became exasperated and angry, and these feelings intertwined with the sight of his bruised cheek, made me recoil in shame. Some days, I couldn't even bear to look him in the eyes and our only interaction was when I tended to the wound.

"You should've called the police then and there," Lucien reprimanded me one day over the telephone. He interrogated Matthew about the assailant (what did he look like? what did he wear?), but it was no use.

It was too dark, Matthew had said numbly.

Lucien called me every day, updating me about his recovery. But Lucien's reprimand pierced me with guilt, and I grew angry at Lucien and Matthew and everyone and everything, even though I knew that Lucien was right. I should have called the police. I should have.

So why didn't I? Why didn't I soften my tone with Matthew? Why didn't I ask him who the perpetrator was? Why couldn't I comfort him when he was most vulnerable? Why was I so useless? I remembered all the times when he made me feel tender and warm, with his fingers stroking through my hair as I cried, and all the times he murmured gentle prayers for the sick birds. The memories made me coil in a ball in my bed, sobbing because for all the times he made me feel loved, like I was floating in our version of paradise, I had been cruel when I should have been kind. Matthew made me feel free and in return I had drowned him.

Most nights, I woke up in dread. In tears. I had a dream where I was alone in the apartment, with the windows wide open as the cold winter air sliced my skin, when an animalistic shriek reverberated through the room, and a flock of white birds flew into the apartment, tearing though the bedsheets and swarming over my head. What I thought was the shrill scream of birds was in fact, my own voice, growing louder and more hysterical until I woke up, gasping for breath.

I couldn't stay in the apartment for much longer.

I threw on my clothes and ran out, slamming the door behind me. The sun shone relentlessly into my eyes but I walked faster and faster. I circled around the market, the parks, anywhere but the apartment. An old man bumped into me and cursed. I couldn't even look him in the eyes as I apologised profusely and hurried off, embarrassed and scared of further rebuke. My step quickened. Suddenly, a loud sharp ring came from my phone. Lucien. When I answered it, my heart sank. Lucien, whose voice was characteristically demanding and controlled, now contorted into anxious urgency.

"Elaine. He's not here. I don't know where he is but he's not here. I waited for three hours and he hasn't come back to the apartment. Look, we had a fight this morning but it was little, and we fight all the time because you know how he gets into his tempers. God Elaine, it was just a small fight. I really didn't think it was—"

I couldn't bear hearing him talk. It made me sick and I hung up the phone, and began running back to the apartment, heart clattering against my chest, my head spinning with morbid scenarios that loomed and threatened with intense clarity. There were flashes of dead white birds and open windows and an empty apartment.

I ripped open the door, ran into the hallway, yelling Matthew's name again and again, my vision dizzy and my voice, hoarse and delirious.

"Matthew, please. God Matthew, I'm so sorry." I was wailing, and terror threatened to overwhelm me as each room— the kitchen, the bathroom— revealed nothing. Like no one had lived there. Like it would never house anyone ever again.

The last room I entered was our bedroom and by then, I was flailing and sputtering. When I opened the door, I was greeted with a violent rush of wind from the open window. And tucked in the corner of the room like a little child, was Matthew, hands around his knees, rocking back and forth. He was so thin and hollow in that white shirt, like he would fall and crumple at any moment.

I ran and collapsed into him, tears streaming down my face, my whole body shaking from nerves.

"I'm so sorry, Matthew. Please forgive me." I was unsure if he said anything, but I repeated it again and again, afraid he didn't hear me the first time. But of course, he did because his fingers fell softly on my hair and stroked it like he always did when I cried. He had uttered his forgiveness without words. He had prayed for me like I was a wounded bird. Soundless and sincere. My cruelty softened.

We sat there for a long time, hands wrapped around each other, resembling one singular entity. My breathing slowed. I looked him in the eye again. Even touched his cheek.

I returned to him. I returned to myself.

I knew that finally, I could return to the apartment; to our apartment, where every morning, sunlight streaked through the gauze-like curtains and Matthew rose out of bed to watch the white birds float from the sky to the pavement, settling there like small marble saints.

**Elias Hart** - *Melbourne, VIC*
*My name is Elias Hart (a pen name), and I am a writer located in Melbourne Australia, currently studying at The University of Melbourne. I enjoy the art of writing as a medium to explore characters and emotions.*

# 23

## *Vicki Renner*

### THE REAL BEE

No one remembers the bees. The real bees. No one except me and Timo.

No one remembers the big fluffy ones, looping through the air like yellow and black teddy bears. Or the blue banded ones only found in Australia, looking like miniature pom poms. No one even remembers the fat European ones that used to float lazily above flowers like tiny blimps. The tiny native ones with their almost invisible antennae. The golden honey bees with their feet yellow and their bodies heavy with pollen. Our memories are their final resting place.

Until today.

I remember these beings – and many more – from my days as a child, in the gardens, before glass, metal, and nanoskin covered the growing zones to protect them from the raging heat and destructive rains.

Until today, the old bees had been a distant memory.

For nearly a century, the gardens I've managed have been filled with the whine of mechanical bees, dutifully fulfilling their job of pollination. Designed in mech warehouses and built by AI-powered machinery for just one purpose: to keep humans alive. These robobees are never born. They are constructed from nanofibres and tiny pieces of metal and miniscule elements of code. They don't live and they don't die. They don't float through the sky, experiencing the wind and the warmth and the rain. They don't gently feel their way along petals like a dancer tiptoeing across the stage; they know exactly where and for how long to dip their metal proboscis into the hearts of the tiny white carrot flowers. They don't even make honey. That is fabricated inside steel towers filled with clanking machinery, devoid of pollen.

Robobees know nothing of intricate hives, the drive to procreate, or even the death that comes after a sting.

Their mechanised motions emit a single-tone whine that I've filtered out over the years. After ninety-five years managing this garden of carrots, parsnips, turnips, and beetroot, my movements are as mechanical and monotone as the robobees, as I perform my row-by-row tasks of monitoring and measuring and data collecting. So this morning when I walked down Row M127 and heard the haphazard humming off to my left, at first I didn't stop. My feet, mind and hands did what they've always done, and I kept walking. But the humming didn't cease, and finally, after a space of time that I can't measure, I heard it. A thrilling sound, delicate and wild and unpredictable. I stopped walking, measuring, monitoring. For the first time in decades.

My body trembled as I reached out through the air with my ears.

I stood still for too long, and Timo's voice projected through the garden.

"Jeannie, get moving! You're not paid to stand still."

The wild humming soared close to my ear, and I felt a swish of air from its tiny wings. I spun on the spot, churning the fine-ground mulch on the floor, searching with eyes, ears, and heart.

"Timo, can you hear it? Come down here and listen."

"If I come down, it will be to call the medics for an assessment. If you're hearing things that don't exist, you're of no use."

The humming thing whizzed past me, in front of my eyes. Chaotic and wild, bobbing up and down, not flying in a straight line along the row of carrot tops. It was a blur of black and gold, as if part of the sun had become detached and was flitting around the garden. Something scratched my right cheek, a shivering sensation as fleeting as it was soft.

"Did you see it!?" I cried.

Nothing from Timo, and I assumed he was watching and listening, that he'd seen the bee or heard it. Then the mechanical gates at the end of the garden opened. The huge gates that are only opened to let me in and out.

Within seconds he was in front of me, his old lined face worried and concerned and kind.

"Jeannie, you know the rules. Thousands of people rely on the food we grow here. They rely on you having all your senses. If you're starting to hear and see things that aren't there, we have to run tests." His voice was deliberately calm. Which meant he'd already made up his mind.

"No, Timo, please! There's a real bee in here. Don't you remember what they sounded like? I can hear its wings, carrying it all over the place."

"Oh Jeannie, you've been at this job longer than any before you. It's a badge of pride, and you'll receive a retirement worthy of your contribution. Why hold on for longer than you need to?"

"I know what I heard, Timo. I know what I felt against my skin."

"You felt a bee crawling on you?" He smirked. Ah yes. That's the start. The smirking and the snide comments. The beginning of the end for an old person.

"I heard it, Timo. You have to believe me. A real bee. The sound was so different from the mechanical whine of robobees; this was random, multi-pitched, shifting in volume and tone."

"You know as well as I do that bees no longer exist. They're all gone. Perhaps you're remembering something from childhood."

"I'm not going senile! I know what I heard and saw!" I shouted at him. I've never shouted in the garden before and we both froze for a moment.

Shock raced across his face before he said quietly and firmly, "We must release the bees. If you won't, then I will."

"No! If you release the robobees, the real one will die!"

"Oh my god, Jeannie, I'm taking charge now. You're finished. Your retirement starts—" Then he stopped, tilted his head, his eyes suddenly wide.

And I knew he'd heard it. The wild, haphazard humming.

"You can't let the robobees in."

He said nothing and I saw a hardness descend upon him. His edges became sharper, his eyes narrower, his mouth tighter.

"Time for you to leave."

"But Timo!" I cried, wrestling my arm out of his grip. "You heard it too!"

"I heard nothing but your voice, whining in my head."

"Don't you get it!? We have a chance, like none have had for decades."

"What are you talk—

"We have the chance to bring something back."

I saw in his face, the way it twisted back on itself, as if his mouth was trying to consume his chin, that he knew; he'd heard the bee. He knew what it was.

"Don't you remember what it was like? To be in a real garden, surrounded by flowers and birds and bees?" He hesitated. I watched him remember what it was like to be a gardener, in the days before the collapse. What it felt like to shove his rake into the earth and lift up potatoes, to snap peas in front of his nose, to pluck a peach off the tree and crunch into it before it was truly ripe. I remembered too, because I was there, by his side, in the dying days of the old world.

Then his face closed over and he grabbed my arm.

"Jeannie, we have no choice."

"No!" I cried, ugly with grief and fear. "You can't!"

He dragged me out of the garden, through the soaring metal gates, and as he entered the code for the doors to close, I struggled and screamed. I don't know why it mattered so much to me. But the thought of that lone tiny insect being trapped with thousands of mechanised creatures filled me with dread.

The guttural shriek of the gates tore into me as they swung shut.

The single note of thousands of mechanical bees erupted, loud and deafening even through the metal doors. The perfectly ordered lines of bees like tiny soldiers, regimented and controlled, streamed down from the top of the dome.

I wanted the madness of that chaotic lone bee. That gold and black creature, made of blood and a heart and a brain. But I knew it was being torn to pieces inside the garden, unable to withstand the sharp edges of the robobees and their metal wings.

Timo left me there, gazing into the garden that had been my home for so long. It would never be the same again.

As his footsteps drifted away, I was left alone. That's when I heard the sound.

Beside my ear. A sudden chaotic humming.

Something soft brushed my cheek.

A blur of gold and black floated past the corner of my eye, finding its way through the air. Beyond the gates.

**Vicki Renner** has been writing since she discovered poetry at the age of 9, finding her voice through a Wordsworth-inspired poem. Now she writes novels and short stories into which she pours her passion for words, characters, other worlds, and the Earth and its creatures.

# 24

# *Angus Clark*

## SUNLIGHT

Sunset ripples over
    Whipped cream curls crashing
Upon a shore of glassy golden syrup

Gentle rays touch down,
Dancing with flicking swirls of sand,
Leaving footprints barely indented.

Spying the secrets of the sunset farewell,
A child hides in the dunes,
Hoping to catch the Pale's greetings.

# MOONLIGHT

Plump leafy crowds sway,
    Liquid onyx washes up foamy forms,
And twinkling judges open their eyes

From behind a torn grey curtain,
White beams glide down, setting the greyscale stage
For dancing water nymphs and swooping seagulls

As colour seeps back in from afar –
Sleepy now in silky dunes –
The child grins at winking stars

*__Angus Clark__ is a writer based in Melbourne, VIC. Angus is a recently graduated creative writer dedicated to revitalising the literary scene wherever he is through The Provocative Inklings, of which he is a co-founder. He is always scribbling in his writer journals.*

## Words of a Feather

Words of a Feather is a studio for young* writers of all ages, based in Melbourne and online. Founded by Melbourne-based writer Amy Han in 2011, WOAF offers in-person and online creative writing workshops, events, and opportunities for emerging writers, in Melbourne and around the world.
**wordsofafeather.co | @woafie.writers.studio**

## The Provocative Inklings

The Provocative Inklings are a Melbourne writing collective co-founded by two University of Melbourne graduates, Angus Clark and Kartiya Ilardo. They publish journalistic, creative, and multimedia pieces, with their main passion being to create a creative community in Melbourne's literary scene. **@theprovocativeinklings**

Collaboratively, Words of a Feather & The Provocative Inklings lead several ongoing events and opportunities for emerging writers in Melbourne and beyond.
This printed anthology is one of them.

# Praise for Michelle Tang

"In DuMort, Tang uses language like a needle, stitching together patches of loneliness and longing until you're left draped in an ever-shifting quilt of tragedy. Our return to Mydalla is as thrilling as our first glimpse of the suffocating society. There's intrigue. Class warfare. Love lost—or worse, transmutated into something toxic, something cancerous. If all this wasn't striking enough, the final image of DuMort is one that'll stay with me for years to come."

— CHRISTOPHER O'HALLORAN, AUTHOR
OF PUSHING DAISY

"With DuMort, Michelle Tang delivers a stunning work of dystopian gothic fiction, honoring the genre's traditions while interweaving fantastic new threads. Tang conjures a world full of candlelit shadows and whispered secrets, and the novel is impeccably constructed, with lush, evocative prose. Fans looking for more of the eerie elegance of Nosferatu will not be disappointed."

— JOLIE TOOMAJAN, SHIRLEY JACKSON
AWARD-WINNING EDITOR OF ASEPTIC
AND FAINTLY SADISTIC

"Tang's dark, elegant prose is equally at home in the glitz of secret high society gatherings as skulking around the grime of nocturnal alleys in this haunting exploration of the price of regret, the pain of loss, and the lengths one will go to for forgiveness."

— BRETT MITCHELL KENT, AUTHOR OF<br>WHISPER OF APPLE BLOSSOMS

"A haunting tale of loneliness, guilt, and monstrosity, *DuMort* deftly explores the complexities of diaspora identity and the unshackling of societal expectations. With gorgeous prose and a heart-stopping conclusion, Tang's debut novella is absolutely unforgettable."

— KELSEA YU, SHIRLEY JACKSON<br>AWARD-NOMINATED AUTHOR<br>OF *BOUND FEET* AND *DEMON SONG*

"To visit Mydalla is to experience a fully realized world of vindictive shrouds, whispered incantations, and barters of flesh. Truth, like the shadows of grief, are exposed by lantern light, as the silver chariots of an unjust society imprison the tormented. DuMort is Michelle Tang at her best, and solidifies her status as one of the best authors of speculative horror writing today."

— TIMAEUS BLOOM, CO-EDITOR OF<br>HOWLS FROM THE SCENE OF THE<br>CRIME